Chantelle Shaw

DI CESARE'S PREGNANT MISTRESS

EXPECTING!

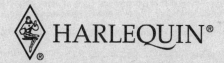

HARLEQUIN®

TORONTO • NEW YORK • LONDON
AMSTERDAM • PARIS • SYDNEY • HAMBURG
STOCKHOLM • ATHENS • TOKYO • MILAN • MADRID
PRAGUE • WARSAW • BUDAPEST • AUCKLAND

ISBN-13: 978-0-373-12727-6
ISBN-10:   0-373-12727-8

DI CESARE'S PREGNANT MISTRESS

First North American Publication 2008.

Copyright © 2008 by Chantelle Shaw.

Printed in U.S.A.

All about the author...
Chantelle Shaw

CHANTELLE SHAW lives on the Kent coast, five minutes from the sea, and does much of her thinking about the characters in her books while walking on the beach. An avid reader from an early age, she found that school friends used to hide their books when she visited, but Chantelle would retreat into her own world, and she still writes stories in her head all the time.

Chantelle has been blissfully married to her own tall, dark and very patient hero for over twenty years and has six children. She began to read Harlequin books as a teenager and throughout the years of being a stay-at-home mom to her brood, she found romance fiction helped her to stay sane!

Her aim is to write books that provide an element of escapism, fun and of course romance for the countless women who juggle work and a home life, and who need their precious moments of "me" time. She enjoys reading and writing about strong-willed, feisty women and even stronger-willed, sexy heroes. Chantelle is at her happiest when writing. She is particularly inspired while cooking dinner, which unfortunately results in a lot of culinary disasters! She also loves gardening, taking her very badly behaved terrier for walks and eating chocolate (followed by more walking—at least the dog is slim!).

CHAPTER ONE

'THAT's Tamsin Stewart—walking into the ballroom now. And there's my father rushing over to her. I can't believe Daddy is making such a fool of himself. She's young enough to be his daughter, for heaven's sake!'

The waspish comment caused Bruno Di Cesare to turn his head and follow Annabel Grainger's gaze across the ballroom to the blonde who had just walked into the room. His first thought was that the woman looked nothing like he had expected, and his eyes narrowed as he lifted his glass to his lips and savoured a mouthful of vintage champagne while he studied her.

When Annabel—younger daughter of his friend and business associate James Grainger—had phoned him and sobbed that her father was involved with a 'bimbo', he'd pictured a brittle bleached blonde wearing some skimpy outfit that revealed acres of overly-tanned flesh. Tamsin Stewart was certainly blonde, but she bore no further similarity to the image in his head.

Her slender figure was emphasised by her silk dress: an elegant, floor-length navy sheath that moulded her breasts and skimmed her flat stomach and the gentle curve of her hips. Her delicate oval face was dominated by huge eyes, although he could not make out their colour from this distance, and her mouth was wide and full and deliciously tempting, coated in a pale pink gloss. Her hair was swept up into a chignon, leaving her long, slender neck exposed, and the ornate diamond necklace she was wearing was almost as eye-catching as the woman herself.

She was beautiful, Bruno conceded, irritated by his reaction to her. The last thing he had expected was to feel physically attracted to a woman he had good evidence to suggest was a callous gold-digger with her sights set on James Grainger's fortune.

Annabel snatched a champagne flute from the bar. 'Look at her—she's all over him,' she muttered disgustedly, downing half the contents of her glass in one gulp.

Bruno reminded himself that Annabel was eighteen now, and entitled to drink alcohol. Over the years that he had been friends with the Graingers he had come to regard her as a little sister, and he frowned at the stark misery on her face.

Across the room Tamsin Stewart was smiling warmly at James as she reached up and brushed a speck of confetti from his jacket. The gesture spoke of an unusual level of intimacy between employer and employee, and Bruno's jaw hardened. Initially he had dismissed Annabel's claim that her father was besotted with a woman half his age. James Grainger was one of the shrewdest businessmen Bruno had ever met, and for the last eighteen months had been grieving the death of his adored wife. It was impossible to imagine him starting a relationship with any woman—especially one who was the same age as one of his daughters.

Nevertheless, Bruno had requested a report on Miss Stewart from one of his many contacts, and he had been sufficiently concerned by what he'd learned to cancel a trip to the US and fly to England to attend James daughter's wedding.

The marriage of Earl Grainger's eldest daughter, Lady Davina, to the Right Honourable Hugo Havistock had taken place in the private chapel on the Grainger estate, followed by a sit-down meal for family members and close friends at a nearby hotel. Now another two hundred guests had arrived at the Royal Cheshunt for the evening reception, and Tamsin Stewart was one of them.

Annabel watched her father lead the beautiful blonde onto the dance floor, and then rounded on Bruno. 'You see! I'm not imagining things,' she said angrily. 'Tamsin seems to have *bewitched* my father.'

'If that's the case, then we will just have to find a way to release him from her spell, *piccola*,' Bruno murmured softly.

Annabel stared at him. 'But how can we?' Her face clouded. 'I thought Daddy had bought that necklace for me,' she choked, lifting her glass to her lips to take another long sip of champagne.

Frowning, Bruno glanced at the diamonds around Tamsin Stewart's swan-like neck.

'Daddy bought all the bridesmaids one of these,' Annabel muttered, fingering the string of pearls at her throat, 'but when I was tidying his study—' she flushed faintly '—I found the diamond necklace and thought he was going to give it to me. I am the chief bridesmaid, after all,' she added sulkily. 'I couldn't believe it when he said it was for Tamsin, in thanks for her work on Davina's flat.'

'If only he hadn't decided to employ an interior designer as part of Davina and Hugo's wedding present, he would never have met her,' Annabel continued dolefully. 'Davina thinks Daddy is lonely, and just wants someone to talk to, but she's been so wrapped up in the wedding that she doesn't understand what a hold Tamsin has over him.'

Annabel drained her glass and held it out to the barman to

refill it. 'Oh, Bruno, I don't know what to do. I wouldn't be surprised if Tamsin has set her sights on becoming the next Lady Grainger. Daddy has been so unhappy since Mummy died,' she said thickly. 'I couldn't bear it if she hurt him.'

'She won't, *piccola*, because I won't allow her to.'

Bruno caught the shimmer of tears in Annabel's eyes and a hard knot of anger settled in his chest. He had known Annabel and Davina since they were children, when Lorna and James Grainger had welcomed him into their home on his frequent business trips to England. He had been saddened by Lorna's untimely death from cancer, and understood the raw grief of the family she had left behind. He felt protective of Lorna's daughters—and in a strange way of James too, as the older man struggled to come to terms with the loss of his beloved wife.

He took another sip of champagne, following James and Tamsin's progress around the dance floor while he considered what he knew of her. She was twenty-five, and single since her divorce two years ago. After university she had worked for a top London design company, where she had gained a reputation as a talented designer, and she had recently joined her brother's property development and design company, Spectrum.

Almost certainly Tamsin's move to Spectrum would have meant a drop in her salary, but the lady had expensive tastes, and Bruno was curious to know how she had afforded her recently purchased new car and spent two weeks at an exclusive holiday complex in Mauritius—not to mention her penchant for designer clothes. The dress she was wearing tonight was from a well-known fashion house—although not his own, Bruno noted—and he was sure it would have been out of her price range. Someone had bought it for her—and Bruno had a good idea who that someone was.

He knew that James Grainger travelled to London every

week to meet Tamsin. Did she persuade him to take her shopping for clothes and jewellery? Or had she seen the diamond necklace and hinted that she wanted it?

But shopping trips were one thing—investing a huge sum of money in Tamsin's brother's company was quite another, Bruno mused grimly. A month ago Spectrum Development and Design had been facing bankruptcy, but at the last minute James had put a vast amount of money into the company to save it from collapse. Bruno knew for a fact that James's financial advisors had been strongly against the deal, but James had refused to listen.

Sexual attraction could make a fool of even the most astute man, Bruno acknowledged bitterly. His father had proved that when he had married a woman half his age. Miranda had caused Stefano Di Cesare's downfall, both professionally and personally, and—even worse—the vacuous actress with her surgically enhanced figure had engineered a rift between Bruno and his father that had not been resolved before Stefano's death.

He had been in his early twenties when his father had remarried. Old enough and mature enough to want Stefano to be happy, but still grieving for his mother, who had died less than a year earlier. *Dio*, he had tried his best to like Miranda, even though his instincts had warned him she was an avaricious slut. But his instincts had proved right, he thought grimly, and now they were warning him that Tamsin Stewart was another Miranda, playing on the emotions of a vulnerable older man.

Bruno had huge respect for James, and over the years they had done business together they had become close friends. But the similarity between the Earl's and his own father's situation could not be ignored. Stefano had also been a lonely widower, flattered by the attention of a pretty young woman— surely James Grainger had more sense than to lose his head to a blonde sex-pot?

Across the room, Tamsin Stewart was laughing with James, her lovely face animated and her eyes sparkling as they shared a private joke, seeming oblivious to the other dancers around them.

Annabel stared at them for a moment, scowling. 'She was married to the brother of one of my friends, you know,' she muttered. 'Caroline told me how she blatantly targeted Neil once she knew that he was a successful businessman earning a fortune in the city. Apparently Neil realised he'd made a mistake soon after they married—when Tamsin moaned about his long working hours but was happy to spend his money. But when he tried to end their relationship, she told him she was pregnant—presumably to make him stay with her.'

'So she has a child?' Bruno queried sharply.

'Oh, no,' Annabel replied. 'Neil divorced her, and I don't know what happened about the baby. Caroline thinks Tamsin may have made up the story about being pregnant, but it didn't work. As I said, Neil insisted on a divorce, and Caro thinks he's well shot of her.

'Daddy's latest idea is to have Ditton Hall completely re-furbished,' she said dully. 'Even though Mummy loved it the way it is. And he's going to ask Tamsin to design it. Daddy says that we have to accept Mummy's gone and move on, but I couldn't bear it if Tamsin moved into Ditton Hall. I'd have to move out and live on the streets or something.'

The idea of spoilt, pampered Annabel living rough was laughable, but Bruno caught the note of real misery in her voice and his anger intensified. The young girl had been dev-astated by her mother's death, and was understandably hurt and dismayed by her father's relationship with Tamsin Stewart.

His mouth compressed into a hard line as he moved lithely towards the dance floor, tugging Annabel after him. 'Your father would never do anything to upset you, and he certainly wouldn't want you to leave Ditton Hall,' he reassured her. 'Now I think it's time you introduced me to the lovely Miss Stewart.'

Tamsin glanced at James Grainger and frowned when she noted the greyish tinge to his skin. He looked drained, she thought worriedly. 'After this dance I think you should sit down and rest. You must have been on your feet for most of the day, and you know what the doctor said about getting too tired,' she told him firmly.

James chuckled, but did not argue with her. 'Yes, Nurse. You sound as bossy as my wife—and that's saying something.' His smile faded and a flash of pain crossed his face. 'Lorna would have been in her element today, organising everything. She'd have loved it.'

'I know,' Tamsin said softly. 'But you've done a wonderful job with this wedding. Davina looks so happy, and I'm sure that neither of the girls has guessed.' She bit her lip and then murmured, 'But, James, I really think you should tell them— if not now, then after Davina and Hugo get back from their honeymoon.'

'No.' James Grainger shook his head fiercely. 'Eighteen months ago they lost their mother to cancer. There's no way I'm going to tell them I've been diagnosed with the same disease. Not yet anyway,' he added, when Tamsin opened her mouth to argue. 'Not until I've seen the specialist again and discussed my prognosis. I don't want to worry them unnecessarily. Annabel is only eighteen, and she's too young to have to deal with any more traumas. Promise me you won't say anything to the girls or anyone else?' he pleaded.

Tamsin nodded reluctantly. 'Of course I won't, if that's what you want. But I'm coming to the hospital with you on Friday. The chemotherapy made you so sick last time.' She paused before adding hesitantly, 'I could be wrong, but I get the feeling that Annabel isn't happy about us meeting—especially now you can no longer pretend we're discussing my designs for Davina's flat. If she knew your trips to London are to the hospital…'

'No,' James insisted again. 'She'd be scared witless. Anyway,' he added cheerfully, 'I've told her I'm meeting you to discuss ideas for refurbishing Ditton Hall.'

'Yes,' Tamsin said slowly, 'I'm afraid that's what's upset her.'

But what could she do about the situation? Tamsin fretted. She had first met James Grainger when she had been commissioned to design Davina and Hugo's flat, and had quickly realised that beneath James's friendly charm was a man teetering on the edge of despair at the loss of his wife.

Tamsin had sympathised with James, and understood his reluctance to burden his daughters with his misery when they were grieving for their mother. And so she had taken time to chat to him whenever they had met at the flat, and had gently encouraged him to talk about Lorna Grainger.

A deep friendship had developed between them, and James had confided in her when he'd gone for tests to determine if he had prostate cancer. Since the diagnosis she had faithfully kept his secret, but she had been unable to persuade him to reveal the truth to Davina and Annabel. And now she had a feeling that Annabel resented her friendship with James.

Sighing, she let her fingers stray to her neck, nervously checking the diamond necklace that hung like a heavy weight around her throat.

'Stop fiddling with it. It's fine,' James chided her.

'I'm terrified I'll lose it. I really think I should take it off and return it to you.'

'I've told you, I don't want it back. It's a present.'

'And I told you I can't accept it,' Tamsin told him firmly.

'Please understand. It must be worth a fortune, and it wouldn't be…appropriate for me to keep it.'

'I just wanted to thank you for your support these past few months by giving you something special for your birthday,' James said stubbornly. 'I don't know what I would have done without you. Lorna would have liked you,' he added gruffly.

The sadness in his eyes brought a lump to Tamsin's throat, and on impulse she leaned up and kissed him lightly on the cheek. 'I help because we're friends, and I certainly don't want you to repay me with expensive jewellery.' She gave the older man a rueful look, knowing that he would be deeply hurt if she insisted on returning the necklace. 'But thank you—the necklace is beautiful and I'll treasure it.'

'Daddy, you haven't danced with me once this evening.'

At the sound of the faintly petulant voice, Tamsin glanced round. Her heart sank when she saw Annabel Grainger staring sulkily at her. She quickly stepped away from James, feeling guilty that she had monopolised his attention. But as she swung round to walk off the dance floor she cannoned into a hard wall of muscle encased in silk—and when she lifted her head her eyes meshed with the midnight-dark gaze of Annabel's partner.

Her first thought was that she had never in her life seen a man like him. His stunning looks stole the breath from her body, and as his eyes locked with hers she stood stock-still and simply stared at him, absorbing the impact of his perfectly sculpted bone structure and the dark olive skin stretched taut over his high cheekbones. His jaw was square, and hinted at an implacable determination to always get his own way, but his mouth was wide and sensual, and Tamsin felt a curious longing to trace the full curve of his upper lip with her fingers.

Awareness seeped through her veins until her body throbbed with a slow, deep yearning that began in the pit of her stomach and radiated out, weakening her limbs with a desire that was shockingly fierce and utterly unexpected. The gleam in his ebony eyes warned her that he knew what she was thinking, and her face burned. Hopefully not *exactly* what she was thinking, she prayed fervently, and she hastily banished the fantasy of him carrying her off to the nearest empty room and making passionate love to her.

Tension coiled in the pit of her stomach, and heat suffused her whole body so that she was sure her face must be scarlet. He was exceptionally tall, sheathed in an expertly cut dark grey suit that emphasised his height and the width of his shoulders, and even when she stepped away from him, mumbling an apology, she felt overwhelmed by his powerful masculinity.

'Forgive me, pumpkin, but I thought you were enjoying yourself with your friends,' James apologised to his daughter. 'Have you been taking care of my little girl, Bruno?'

'Of course,' the man replied smoothly. 'But you know, James, now that Davina is married, and about to leave Ditton Hall, I think Annabel feels in need of her *papà*.' His accent was unmistakably Italian, his voice as rich and thick as clotted cream, but Tamsin caught his faintly reproving tone and James must have detected it too.

'Come and dance with me, then, darling,' he said jovially. 'Tamsin, do you mind if we swap partners? I have it on good authority that Bruno is an excellent dancer.'

An awkward silence followed, and Tamsin stiffened, unable to bring herself to meet the man's gaze. His close proximity was actually making her tremble, and she was terrified that if she danced with him he would realise the effect he had on her. 'I think I'll sit this one out,' she mumbled, keeping her eyes on James. 'You go ahead.'

James shook his head. 'For heaven's sake, where are my

manners? I haven't even introduced you. Tamsin, this is Bruno Di Cesare—head of the House of Di Cesare fashion empire, and a very good friend. Bruno, may I introduce you to Tamsin Stewart? Tamsin is an amazingly talented interior designer.'

Annabel made an impatient noise and tugged her father's arm. 'Come on, Daddy. I want a drink,' she said loudly, but Tamsin barely heard her, or noticed when James escorted his daughter over to the bar. The music and the other guests on the dance floor faded to the periphery of her mind, and she felt as though only she and Bruno Di Cesare existed.

'Miss Stewart.'

His voice seemed to have dropped several degrees, and his coolness sent an involuntary shiver down Tamsin's spine. Perhaps it was his height that made him seem so intimidating, or maybe it was the hardness of his features and the slightly cynical curl of his lip that made her feel uneasy. She gasped when he suddenly extended his hand and enfolded her fingers in his firm grasp.

'Or may I call you Tamsin?'

He rolled her name on his tongue as if he was savouring a fine wine, and lifted her hand to graze his lips across her knuckles, causing an electrical current to shoot from her fingers along every nerve-ending to her toes. His eyes glinted with amusement when she blushed, and she hated the fact that he clearly knew how much he affected her.

'I hope I can persuade you to dance with me,' he murmured in his sinfully sexy accent, and there was no hint of coolness in his voice now, making her wonder if she had imagined it.

Tamsin had a feeling that he could persuade her to do anything he liked. His smile did strange things to her insides and she felt hot and flustered. He was beautiful, she thought helplessly. She hadn't felt like this since…ever. Not even when she had met her husband.

She'd been attracted to Neil, of course, and as their court-ship had progressed she had fallen in love with him. But she had never experienced this incredible, almost primal sexual awareness that was now pounding through her veins.

At school she'd always been too engrossed in her studies to suffer the same teenage crushes on pop stars or boys in the sixth form which had affected her friends. Her life had been mapped out: qualifications, a career, marriage and babies. But her dreams had been shattered by Neil's infidelity. Her personal life had imploded, and she no longer knew what she wanted, but she suddenly found that she wanted to do something utterly crazy—like fling herself into the arms of this sexy stranger and press her lips against the sensual curve of his mouth.

With a jolt she realised that she was staring at Bruno Di Cesare, and she blushed. She was acting like a teenager on her first date, she told herself irritably, and with a huge effort she returned his smile and strove to sound cool as she murmured, 'Thank you—I'd love to dance.'

She followed him onto the dance floor and a quiver ran through her when he retained his hold on her hand and slid his other arm around her waist, drawing her against the solid muscles of his thighs. She could feel the heat that emanated from his body, and the exotic, musky scent of his cologne swamped her senses. Each of her nerve-endings seemed acutely sensitive, and to her horror she felt a tingling in her breasts as her nipples hardened and strained against the silky material of her dress.

Bruno felt the signals Tamsin's body was sending out and his eyes narrowed on her flushed face. A few moments ago, before James had introduced them, she had been coolly dis-missive of him. But now that she knew he headed a globally successful business empire she was no longer dismissive, but soft and pliant in his arms, with the tip of her pink tongue tracing the shape of her bottom lip in a deliberate invitation that triggered an instant response low in his pelvis.

Money was a powerful aphrodisiac, he thought sardonically. He acknowledged his good-looks without conceit, but knew that even without his classical bone structure and athletic build his wealth ensured that, where women were concerned, he never had to try very hard. Sometimes he wondered if life would be more exciting if he did. He dismissed the thought with a faint shrug and watched Tamsin Stewart's pupils dilate when he smiled at her. It was a clever trick, and he guessed that behind the façade of wide-eyed *ingénue* she was a clever lady.

She was beautiful, but flawed, he reminded himself grimly. A gold-digger with her greedy eyes focused on James Grainger's fortune. He was convinced that she was a woman like his stepmother—a parasite who hoped to worm her way into the heart of a grieving older man and no doubt bleed him dry. But although his brain felt nothing but contempt for her, his body was not so fussy, and he felt an unmistakable tightening in his gut as he imagined crushing her soft pink lips beneath his and removing her dress to tease her tight, swollen nipples with his tongue.

His desire for her was an irritating complication, but it seemed that Tamsin Stewart was equally aware of the chemistry between them. Bruno's jaw tightened and his lips curled into a cruel line. He had been unable to save his father from Miranda's grasping clutches, but no way would he stand back and watch James make the same mistake, he vowed grimly.

Cold, contemptuous anger solidified in his chest as he stared at the array of diamonds around Tamsin's neck and assessed how much the necklace James had given her was worth. He could not believe that the beautiful blonde was interested in a man old enough to be her father for any other reason than that

James was extremely rich. But her undisguised awareness of him provided him with an ideal weapon to foil her plans—and he would have no compunction in using it.

CHAPTER TWO

'SO YOU are an interior designer? Annabel told me you recently completed work on Davina and Hugo's flat,' Bruno said, dipping his head so close to Tamsin's that his warm breath fanned her cheek.

'Yes,' she murmured distractedly, as she attempted to ease away from him a fraction. She felt his hand tighten on her hip so his pelvis rubbed sinuously against hers. Her thought process seemed to have deserted her, and she regretted drinking the glass of champagne she had been presented with when she had first arrived at the reception. Surely it was the alcohol that was making her head swim, rather than the intoxicating presence of the man who was holding her against his broad, muscular chest?

She wondered with a sinking feeling what else Annabel had said about her. Davina's sister had never been particularly friendly towards her—but that was hardly surprising when she was a close friend of Tamsin's ex-sister-in-law, Caroline Harper. Caroline had disliked her on sight, and had bitterly resented Tamsin's presence in Neil Harper's life. Tamsin had understood that Caroline's fractured childhood and her parents' acrimonious divorce had led her to cling to her older brother, but her jealousy had been one of many factors that had driven Neil and Tamsin apart.

'I was honoured when James appointed me to design the flat,' she explained, lifting clear blue eyes to Bruno and smiling at him. 'It's Davina and Hugo's first home as a married couple, and I wanted it to be special.'

And, of course, it had given her an opportunity to ingratiate herself with an extremely wealthy man, Bruno mused cynically, irritated to discover that Tamsin's eyes reminded him of the cobalt Tuscan sky on a summer's day. James Grainger inhabited the rarefied world of the aristocracy, and spent most of his time at his country estate or his gentlemen's club. If it had not been for the commission Tamsin would never have met James, and she had obviously made the most of her luck.

'So, have you only known the Graingers since you won the commission?' he queried.

His sexy smile made it hard for Tamsin to think straight, but she detected a slight nuance in his voice that puzzled her, and she wondered why he was so interested in her relationship with the family.

'Yes. As you can imagine, I worked very closely with Davina and Hugo, and I'm pleased so say they loved my designs. We became friends, and they asked me to their reception tonight.'

'And I understand from Annabel that you are also friendly with James?'

Bruno's expression was bland, but once again Tamsin detected the faint note of censure in his tone. She decided she'd had enough of playing twenty questions. 'James Grainger is charming, and I would like to think we are friends.' She flushed guiltily as she remembered her promise to James that she would not reveal his secret to anyone. She guessed that Bruno was unaware of James's health problems, and it was not her place to tell him. 'We met a few times when he came up to inspect my work on the flat, and on a couple of occasions we had lunch.' She faltered when Bruno regarded her steadily with his unfathomable dark eyes. 'I think James is lonely since he lost his wife,' she added. 'He seemed to want to talk about her.'

'And I'm sure you offered a sympathetic shoulder for him to cry on,' Bruno drawled softly.

While Tamsin was trying to work out quite what he meant by that statement, or if he had even meant anything at all, he trailed a long, tanned finger down her cheek and rested it lightly on the diamond necklace around her throat.

'This is almost as exquisite as the woman wearing it,' he murmured, the sensual gleam in his dark eyes causing Tamsin to catch her breath. 'You have superb taste, *bella,* to have chosen such a beautifully crafted piece of jewellery.'

'Oh, I didn't buy it…it was a present.' Tamsin hesitated; there was no reason why she should not say that the necklace had been a birthday present from James, but she had a strange feeling that Bruno would question why the Earl had given her such an expensive gift. It would be impossible to explain that James had wanted to thank her for the hours she'd sat in the hospital waiting room with him without revealing his secret.

Was it her imagination, or had the stunning Italian's face hardened fractionally behind his smile? Although once again his voice was as seductive as molten syrup as he queried mildly, 'A present from your lover, I suppose?'

He had to be teasing her, didn't he? The look of disappointment on his face couldn't be real. But the warmth of his body pressed close up against hers and the strength of his arms as they tightened round her waist were very real, and Tamsin shook her head dazedly. Common sense told her that a man as gorgeous as Bruno Di Cesare could not really be interested in her. But she remembered how their eyes had locked when she had first stumbled against him on the dance floor, and she recalled her instant and overwhelming feeling that she had known him for eternity. Was it possible that he had been over-whelmed too?

'I don't have a lover,' she whispered, unable to tear her eyes from the sensual curve of his mouth.

'I find that hard to believe, *cara*.' Bruno's velvety voice caressed her and he moved his head even closer to hers, so that his jaw brushed against her cheek. 'But perhaps whoever gave you the necklace hopes to be your lover?'

'No,' she denied sharply, jerking her head back. James was a dear friend who was still grieving the loss of his wife, and the idea that he had given her the necklace for any other reason than friendship was horrible. She didn't understand why Bruno was so interested in the wretched necklace anyway.

When she tried to step away from him he drew her inex-orably closer, so that she could feel the hardness of his thighs pressed against hers. 'I'm not involved with anyone right now. Does that satisfy your curiosity?' He unsettled her, but before she could demand that he release her, he tightened his arms around her.

'Absolutely,' he growled, in a low, intense tone that made the hairs on the back of her neck stand on end. 'And I am relieved that you are not involved with another man, Tamsin, because it means that you are free to become involved with me.'

'Wh…what?' she said, stunned. 'We don't know one another. We only met five minutes ago.'

'But the attraction between us was instant,' Bruno stated coolly, the glint in his eyes daring her to deny it. 'Sexual alchemy at its most potent.'

As if to prove his point, he slid his hand down her back until it rested at the very base of her spine, and then exerted pressure so she was forced into even closer contact with his blatantly aroused body. His action should have appalled her, but to Tamsin's shame all she could think was that their clothes were an unwelcome barrier, and that she longed to feel his warm, naked flesh pressed against hers.

'Lust is such an honest sentiment, don't you think?' he murmured, in his deep, sexy voice that alone had the power to bring her skin out in goosebumps. 'The chemistry that exists between a man and a woman. I want you and you want me—what could be simpler or more honest than that?'

It would be very easy to be swept away by Bruno Di Cesare's sultry charm, Tamsin acknowledged. If she was honest, part of her longed to succumb to his magnetism and follow blindly wherever he led—which, from the sexual heat in his gaze, would, she guessed, be straight to his bed. But some deeply ingrained instinct for self-protection warned her that she would be way out of her depth. She had never met a man like Bruno before. In the two years since her divorce she hadn't even been on a date, and although she could not deny that she was attracted to him, experience had taught her to be cautious.

Fortunately there was a lull in the music, and she stepped firmly out of his arms. Across the room she saw James walking into the adjoining banqueting suite, and she gave Bruno a cool smile. 'I think I'm going to investigate the buffet, *signor*,' she said steadily. 'The sandwiches I bought at the service station on the way down were inedible, and I'm starving. I'm sure you'll have no trouble in finding another dance partner,' she added dryly. She had been aware of numerous pairs of female eyes following Bruno around the dance floor, and knew that the moment she walked away from him there would be a scramble for his attention.

He glanced across the room, following her gaze over to James before his eyes settled once more on her face, and for a split second she thought she glimpsed a look of icy contempt in the dark depths. But then he smiled, and she guessed she must have imagined it. He released her, but remained close by her side as she walked through into the banqueting suite, where a buffet table ran the length of one wall.

'Forgive my impatience, Tamsin,' he apologised huskily, when she frowned at him. 'I'm afraid I've offended you. But my only excuse is that your loveliness takes my breath away.' He handed her a plate and glanced at the wonderful variety of canapés and finger foods displayed in front of them. 'I hope you will allow me to join you?' he begged with exquisite politeness, but his eyes gleamed wickedly when he added dulcetly, 'I suddenly find that I too am starving, *bella*.'

Tamsin's lips twitched. He was an incorrigible flirt who could charm the birds from the trees, but common sense told her that his flattery was all part of a game he was playing. She was reasonably attractive, but there were other, far more beautiful women here tonight, and she could not believe he was seriously interested in her. She helped herself to a couple of blinis topped with cream cheese and smoked salmon, and glanced at him, her pulse-rate quickening when she found his eyes on her. Electricity fizzed between them, shockingly fierce, and she quickly looked away and stared blindly at the food on the table, discovering that her appetite had deserted her.

Bruno Di Cesare was a playboy, she reminded herself as she recalled what she knew of him. She preferred the business section of the newspapers to the gossip columns, but the president of The House of Di Cesare frequently featured in both. She'd read that the company had been created eighty years ago by Antonio Di Cesare, to produce expertly crafted leather goods. Over the years it had diversified to become an iconic fashion house, and had also cornered a worldwide market in top-quality household goods—everything from exquisitely designed sofas and dining tables to the china and glassware that graced the tables of those wealthy enough to afford them. The main outlet for the Di Cesare brand in the UK was Grainger's department store in Knightsbridge, which would explain Bruno's friendship with James Grainger.

Bruno inhabited a different world from hers. He was a billionaire—admired by his peers for his ruthlessness in the boardroom, and by his numerous lovers for his prowess in the bedroom. He was used to having whatever he wanted, whether it involved business or a woman, but if he thought he could simply click his fingers and have her, he was going to be disappointed, Tamsin vowed firmly.

James Grainger was sitting at one of the tables arranged around the room, and once Tamsin had selected her food she started to make her way towards him. But Bruno was instantly at her side, steering her determinedly over to an empty table in a secluded corner. Before she could remonstrate, he took her plate, set it down on the table, and drew out a chair for her to sit down. A waiter materialised with a bottle of champagne in an ice bucket. Bruno filled two glasses, handed her one, then raised his own, his smile revealing a set of perfect teeth that gleamed white against his olive skin. For some reason Tamsin was reminded of a wolf preparing to devour its prey, and a faint prickle of unease feathered down her spine.

'What shall we drink to Tamsin? To us, as we set out on a journey to see where this sexual awareness between us might lead?'

'Certainly not,' Tamsin replied quickly. 'We ought to toast the bride and groom and wish them a long and happy marriage.' Her voice faltered a fraction as she thought of her own failed marriage. Davina and Hugo were so in love that it seemed to radiate from them—but would it last?

Her brief marriage had been a salutary life lesson that had left her heart bruised and her pride in tatters. She had been an impressionable twenty-one-year-old when Neil Harper had swept into her life. She'd fallen in love with the good-looking, ambitious banker, and been overjoyed when he proposed six months later. But the fairy tale had ended a year after their wedding, when he'd left her for a glamorous city trader called Jacqueline.

On her wedding day she had thought that her love for Neil would last a lifetime—and that he loved her with the same intensity, Tamsin remembered sadly. She had believed that her hopes and expectations had been his dreams too, and it had only been afterwards, after he'd moved out on Christmas Eve and told her he was filing for a divorce, that she'd learned he had been sleeping with Jacqueline even before the wedding, and that their affair had continued when he and Tamsin had returned from honeymoon. Her marriage had been a sham from the beginning, she acknowledged bleakly, unaware that Bruno was watching the play of emotions on her face.

'Why the frown, *bella*?' he queried. 'Don't you think Davina and Hugo's marriage will last?'

'Oh, I'm sure it will. I certainly hope so, anyway. I'm sure they really love each other.' Tamsin murmured. 'And that's the most important thing, isn't it?'

The sudden huskiness in her voice aroused Bruno's curiosity. 'Is it? I'm afraid I'm not an expert on love and marriage—having experienced neither,' he drawled. 'But experience has taught me that many women regard getting married as a convenient route to financial security—either within the marriage or after, with a hefty divorce settlement.'

Tamsin put down her spinach tartlet, sure that she would choke if she bit into it. 'How horribly cynical you are. I can't believe any woman would marry for financial security. I'm quite sure Davina didn't marry Hugo for his money—and I married because I was in love with my husband, not because of the size of his bank balance.' She stared at him, wondering what he would think if she revealed that her ex-husband was a wealthy banker. Would he refuse to believe she hadn't married Neil for his money?

Bruno glanced at her speculatively. 'Ah, yes, Annabel mentioned you'd been married. But I understand you are now divorced?'

'Yes,' Tamsin said flatly, lowering her gaze and ignoring his querying look. The reasons why her marriage had ended were still painful, and she had no intention of discussing them with a stranger.

Bruno shrugged laconically. 'And yet you are still optimistic that Davina and Hugo's marriage will be successful. I would have thought that after your own failed attempt at marriage you would see the pitfalls in such an outdated institution. Do you really believe it is possible to remain faithful to one person for a lifetime?'

It was clear that he regarded the idea of love and lifelong fidelity as ridiculous, but Tamsin met his gaze steadily and nodded her head. 'Yes, I do. Despite what happened to me, I think marriage is a wonderful institution. I hope that one day I'll meet a man who I can share my life with. And I won't care if he's rich or poor,' she added fiercely, remembering his outrageous statement that most women married for financial gain.

'An admirable sentiment, *bella*,' Bruno said silkily.

Tamsin sounded convincing, but he was still deeply suspicious of her relationship with James Grainger. Annabel had said that Tamsin had received a generous divorce settlement from her ex-husband, so it was little wonder she was such an enthusiastic supporter of marriage. Miranda Maughn had deliberately targeted his father and used all her feminine wiles to tempt him up the aisle. Had Tamsin decided that marrying and divorcing rich men was a viable career option? He could think of no other reason why she had engineered a friendship with a vulnerable man almost forty years older than her.

For the past ten years James had welcomed him into his home and treated him like a son, Bruno mused. Now it was time he repaid the older man's kindness and saved him from the greedy clutches of a callous gold-digger.

He refilled Tamsin's glass with champagne, and dismissed her small protest with a stunning smile that had the desired effect of making her blush. 'You're not driving, are you?' he queried when she lifted the glass to her lips with fingers that noticeably shook. He frowned as a thought suddenly occurred to him. 'Are you staying here, or at Ditton Hall?'

'Oh, here—James did invite me to stay at the Hall,' Tamsin explained, 'but he has a house full of relatives staying for the weekend, and I thought it would be easier if I booked a room here in the hotel. Where are you staying?'

'I also have a room here.' There was no mistaking the sultry gleam in Bruno's eyes as he added, 'Who knows? Perhaps we'll have breakfast together.'

'I think that's extremely unlikely.' Tamsin strove to sound cool, hoping to hide the fact that she was thoroughly flustered that he anticipated them spending the hours before breakfast together—in his bed. He had a nerve, she thought crossly, but she could not repress the tremor that ran through her at the idea of his olive-toned naked limbs entwined with her own paler body as he made love to her.

Bruno sat back in his chair and studied her speculatively over the rim of his glass. She was blushing again, and he watched in fascination as her creamy skin became tinged with pink. The sophisticated women he usually associated with never blushed—but it was a useful trick, he conceded. With her wide eyes and rosy cheeks Tamsin Stewart looked innocent and unworldly, but he doubted she was either. He dropped his gaze deliberately to her breasts, a cynical smile curving his lips as he noted the provocative peaks of her nipples jutting beneath her dress.

Persuading her that he was a better and richer option than the Earl promised to have its compensations, he decided as he shifted in his seat, attempting to ease the ache in his loins.

'Tell me about yourself,' he invited Tamsin when she pushed her plate away, her food barely touched. 'Do you have a family? Brothers and sisters?'

Tamsin wondered why he had asked, as she seriously doubted he was interested in the boring details of her life, but at least making small talk might help her to ignore the smouldering chemical reaction between them that was in danger of combusting. 'I have two sisters, both happily married to my lovely but not very well-off brothers-in-law,' she told him pointedly. 'And one brother, Daniel, who I work for.'

'Ah, yes—Spectrum Development and Design,' Bruno murmured, and once again Tamsin thought she detected a slight nuance in his voice that puzzled her. 'How is business? I understand the property market in England is struggling at the moment?'

'I really only concentrate on the interior design side of the company, while my brother deals with actually buying and selling the properties, but everything seems to be going well,' she replied with a smile. 'Daniel has just bought a penthouse flat in Chelsea that we intend to renovate and sell, and the profit margins are predicted to be good.'

'He must need a large amount of capital for that kind of venture,' Bruno commented. 'Do you have a sympathetic bank? Or help from private investors?'

'Well, we do borrow money from the bank, of course. Though I'm not really sure about private investors,' Tamsin mumbled, her cheeks turning pink. She had only joined

Spectrum a year ago, after gaining valuable experience at another bigger design company. She was concentrating all her efforts on building up the interior design side, and had little to do with the overall running of things.

Bruno was watching her. His dark, unfathomable gaze made her feel uncomfortable, and she quickly changed the subject. 'How about you—do you have a family?'

'My parents are both dead,' Bruno replied. 'I have one sister, who is a couple of years older than Annabel Grainger.'

His jaw tightened as he remembered Jocasta's unhappiness when his father had married Miranda. His stepmother had torn his family apart, he remembered bitterly, his eyes narrowing when Tamsin put her hand to her throat and stroked the diamonds that sparkled against her skin. Stefano had been besotted by his young wife and had given her many pieces of Bruno's mother's jewellery that should have been passed on to Jocasta. Indeed, Bruno had recently paid his stepmother five times the valued price of a ruby necklace and earrings that his mother had worn on her wedding day. He was sure his father had not given away jewels that had a priceless sentimental value to Miranda, but Stefano had died without leaving a will, so his second wife had inherited everything.

Bruno had not cared about the palatial house in Florence, but he had been determined to reclaim his mother's jewellery. Fortunately Miranda needed money to maintain her lavish lifestyle, and had been willing to sell—at a price. His stepmother's greed sickened him, and as he watched Tamsin lovingly caress the necklace James Grainger had given her the bile in his throat threatened to choke him.

'Is something wrong?' Tamsin asked uncertainly. A moment ago Bruno had been smiling at her, but now his mouth was compressed into a thin line and his eyes were hard and cold. He seemed to be lost in his own world and, once again she felt a prickle of unease run through her.

Her voice seemed to drag him back to the present, and he visibly forced himself to relax. But although he smiled warmly at her, Tamsin shivered.

'Everything is fine, *bella*. Would you like more champagne?'

'No, thank you.' She quickly grabbed her glass before he could refill it. She rarely drank alcohol, and her head felt as though it was spinning after the two glasses she had consumed. She glanced over to where James had been sitting, hoping that he wasn't too tired, but he had gone. When she glanced back she found that Bruno was watching her impassively.

'Shall we return to the ballroom?' he said, standing up and drawing her to her feet.

'Please don't feel that you have to remain with me,' Tamsin said, suddenly desperate to escape him. His potent masculinity disturbed her more than she cared to admit, and she needed time to collect her thoughts and control her body's wayward response to him. 'I'm sure you must want to mingle with the other guests.'

'On the contrary, *cara,* there is only one woman I wish to mingle with,' Bruno assured her throatily as they entered the ballroom, and before she could object he drew her into his arms and brought her body into intimate contact with his.

From then on the evening took on a dreamlike quality, with Bruno holding her close, his eyes blazing with undisguised hunger as they drifted slowly around the room. Several times Tamsin caught sight of James Grainger, but when she attempted to step away from Bruno he tightened his hold around her waist and teasingly informed her that he had claimed her for the rest of the night.

'I'd really like a word with James,' she remonstrated. 'I've hardly spoken to him all evening.'

'I think you should leave him to spend time with Annabel,' Bruno replied, a hard edge to his voice. 'She misses her mother terribly, and now that Davina is moving away she is going to need her father more than ever.'

Tamsin thought that Annabel looked perfectly happy, surrounded by a group of her friends, but Bruno was stroking his hand lightly up and down her spine, and she found it difficult to think of anything but the sensuous glide of his fingers. She knew she should stop this madness and demand that he release her, but her tongue seemed to have tied itself in knots and her body had developed a will of its own. Desire unfurled deep within her like the petals of a flower slowly opening, and instead of pushing him away she relaxed and melted into him, so that her pelvis came into direct contact with his. The solid ridge of his arousal was so shockingly hard that she stumbled, and he tightened his arms around her, bringing her into even closer contact with him, his eyes gleaming mockingly from beneath heavy lids when he noted her flushed face.

'Trust me, you're not the only one to be embarrassed,' he muttered self-derisively. 'We need to get out of here—now, *bella*.'

Without another word he gripped her hand, tugging her after him out onto the wide terrace that ran the length of the ballroom. He drew her into a shadowed recess where a profusion of roses and clematis grew against the wall to form a bower. The night air was cool on Tamsin's heated skin and her head spun. That last glass of champagne had been a bad idea, she thought numbly when Bruno turned her to face him. Yet she wasn't drunk on alcohol, but on the heady feeling that she was a desirable woman. After two years of feeling a failure, the scorching sexual hunger in Bruno's gaze restored a little of the pride that Neil had stripped away.

She stared at him, unaware that the half-hopeful, half-uncertain expression in her eyes and the slight tremor of her lower lip made her impossible for him to resist. He muttered something in Italian as he reached for her and hauled her against the hard wall of his chest. Tamsin made no effort to resist him. She seemed to be rooted to the spot, her heart thumping painfully beneath her ribs as he slowly lowered his head.

His lips were warm and firm, demanding a response she was powerless to deny as he slid one hand to her nape, gently tugging her head back so that she was angled to his satisfaction while his mouth continued a sensual assault that left her trembling. He stroked his tongue persuasively against the tremulous line of her lips, insisting she allow him access, until with a little gasp she capitulated and opened her mouth, so that he could thrust deep into her moist inner warmth.

Heat surged through her veins and her breasts felt heavy and ultra-sensitive as the swollen peaks of her nipples jutted to attention, straining against the silky material of her dress. She lost all notion of time and place; she was only aware of the warmth of his skin as she lifted her fingers to trace his jaw, the musky scent of his cologne that swamped her senses. She wanted the kiss to last for ever—wanted him to continue his wicked exploration with his tongue—and needed with an almost desperate urgency to feel his hands on her body. When she leaned into him he curved his fingers possessively around one breast and she moaned softly, but seconds later he drew back and stared down into her desire-darkened eyes, breathing raggedly.

'*Dio bella*, you are a sorceress,' he rasped. He sounded stunned, almost angry, and he gripped her shoulders as if he wanted to thrust her from him.

'Bruno?' Tamsin whispered his name fearfully, wondering why he suddenly looked so furious—wondering if she had done something wrong.

She wasn't very good at this, she acknowledged bleakly. Neil's repeated infidelity throughout their marriage was proof that she did not know how to please a man. Mortified, she tried to jerk away from him, but Bruno tightened his hold and slammed her hard up against him, so that she could feel the erratic thud of his heart beneath her palm.

'This is madness,' he growled in a raw tone. He seemed to be waging a battle with himself, and he was breathing hard as he stared at her upturned face before he lowered his head once more. Their mouths met, fusing with a wildfire passion that was fierce and hot and shockingly primitive. His tongue forced entry between her lips and proceeded to explore her with a thoroughness that left her trembling, her limbs so weak that she clung to his shoulders and anchored her fingers in the silky dark hair at his nape.

Nothing had prepared her for the bolt of white-hot need that ripped through her, scalding her flesh and tossing her doubts and inhibitions aside as if they were flotsam on the tide. She was burning up in the blazing heat of his passion. At last Bruno eased the pressure of his mouth a fraction, and the kiss became a long, unhurried tasting that drugged her senses and stoked her desire, so that her breasts felt full and heavy and ached for his touch.

'My room or yours?' he demanded, barely lifting his mouth from hers.

His harsh, grating voice splintered the soft night air and shattered the spell he had woven around her. Reality reared its unwelcome head, and she stared at him dazedly.

'I…'

'I have to have you, *bella*—tonight.' He had never known such fierce hunger for a woman, and such was his desperation to possess her that he was tempted to carry her into the shadowed grounds and make love to her on the grass.

Somewhere in the recesses of his mind Bruno knew that he had an ulterior motive for persuading Tamsin into his bed. His intention was to persuade her to transfer her attention from James to him—secure in the knowledge that, whilst James might be tempted to fall in love with her, he, Bruno, never would.

But right now nothing seemed more important than assuaging the throbbing ache that consumed him.

'The other guests are starting to leave. No one will notice if we slip away to my suite,' he muttered hoarsely, staring at Tamsin in disbelief when she shook her head and stepped away from him.

'I can't,' she whispered. 'I'm sorry.'

'*Madre de Dio!* Tamsin—'

Bruno's furious voice followed Tamsin as she flew along the terrace and through the doors to the ballroom, her heart beating so hard she was sure it would burst out of her chest.

He was right. Many of the guests were leaving, and only a few couples remained on the dance floor. They would not have been missed. If she had said yes to Bruno's husky request they would already be in his room, and he would be kissing her with the same hungry passion that had overwhelmed them both a few moments ago.

Why hadn't she agreed to go with him? she asked herself angrily. Why hadn't she for once in her life followed the dictates of her body rather than her brain? Bruno had aroused her to such a fever-pitch of desire that every muscle seemed to be screaming with sexual frustration. But the sound of his voice, his confident assumption that she would fall into his bed as readily as she had responded to his kisses, had halted her wanton response to him.

After her disastrous marriage her self-confidence was at rock-bottom, she acknowledged miserably, hurrying out of the

ballroom and across the hotel foyer. She had been flattered
by Bruno's attention and shocked by the feelings he aroused
in her. But she was well aware of his reputation as a woman-
iser. He was a billionaire playboy who was used to women
throwing themselves at him, and her pride refused to allow
her to be just another notch on his bedpost.

'Tamsin, my dear, is everything all right?' James Grainger
emerged from the hotel lounge and Tamsin skidded to a halt
in front of him. 'You look rather flushed.'

'Oh…it was hot in the ballroom, and I think I've had a little
too much champagne,' she said quickly, casting a nervous
glance over her shoulder to see if Bruno had followed her.
'I'm going up to my room now, James—' She broke off and
caught hold of his arm as he swayed unsteadily. 'You don't
look at all well.'

'I'm just tired. It's been a long and emotional day—but a
successful one, I think,' James murmured, giving her a weary
smile. 'Davina and Hugo are on their way to the airport, and
Annabel is still in the bar with her friends. But I'm going back
to the Hall now. Hargreaves is waiting out front with the car.'

'Let me help you.' Without waiting for James to reply,
Tamsin tightened her hold on his arm and urged him to lean
on her as they walked slowly across the foyer. At the top of
the steps he stumbled, and she was glad when his chauffeur
hurried to offer his assistance. 'I'll come and see you
tomorrow,' she promised gently, and James nodded.

'I'd like that. I want to discuss ideas for the house.' He hesitated, and then added in a voice tinged with embarrassment,
'Tamsin, I couldn't help but notice that you seemed rather
taken with Bruno tonight. And there's nothing at all wrong
with that,' he continued swiftly, when she blushed scarlet.
'I've known Bruno for years, and he is a fine, honourable
man—but a man, nevertheless, who has a deserved reputation

as a playboy. Just be careful, hmm?' he said softly as he climbed into the car. 'Goodnight, my dear.'

Bruno walked to the end of the terrace, breathing hard as he sought to bring his body under control. He could think of several words to describe Tamsin Stewart, and none of them pleasant, he thought savagely. Her passionate response to him had stoked his hunger until it was a raging furnace, and her cool rejection had left him in agony. Why had she stopped? Did she take pleasure in teasing men and taking them to the edge? Or had there been another reason why she had walked away from him?

And then, illuminated in the light spilling from the hotel entrance, he saw her with James Grainger—saw James get into his car and realised that Tamsin was about to join him. So that was her game. That was the reason she had refused to go to his room—she was going back to Ditton Hall with James.

With a furious curse Bruno swung round and strode back along the terrace, his body rigid with anger as he heard the car pull away. Davina's wedding must have been an emotive day for James, and he was clearly missing his dead wife, he thought grimly. Tamsin had obviously decided that this was a perfect time to make a move on the Earl—and there wasn't a damn thing he could do to stop her.

CHAPTER THREE

THE following morning Bruno's temper was still simmering dangerously, and his body was aching with the sexual frustration that had kept him awake until the early hours. Failure and rejection were not words he was familiar with, but last night he had experienced both—and he was incensed. Not only had he failed to keep Tamsin away from James Grainger, but she had responded to him with a passion that he had believed matched his own and then turned it off as easily as flicking a light switch, leaving him racked with unfulfilled desire.

His plan to rescue the Earl from her greedy clutches by enticing her into his bed was not proving as easy as he had expected. He was furious that he had not prevented her from accompanying James back to Ditton Hall—and the idea that she might even have spent the night in James's bed made him want to hit something.

Breathing hard, he strode into the dining room—and halted abruptly at the sight of Tamsin sitting alone at a table overlooking the hotel gardens.

In a pink tee shirt and white jeans, with her blonde hair falling around her shoulders like a curtain of silk, she looked young and innocent and at the same time incredibly sexy. The hungry beast that had clawed in Bruno's gut all night stirred into life once more, and his body reacted with irritating pre-dictability as he walked towards her.

'*Buongiorno*. May I join you?'

Tamsin had been watching a sparrow hopping along the terrace, and the sound of Bruno's deep, sexy drawl made her heart plummet. She turned her head and eyed him warily, sure that he must be furious with her for the way she had run from him last night.

'Yes, of course,' she murmured, wondering why he had bothered to ask when he had already sat down at her table. She didn't know what to say to him, and her face burned as she recalled in stark detail the passionate kisses they had exchanged on the moonlit terrace. At the time it had seemed like a dream, but now it was more like a nightmare—especially when she re-membered how fervently she had responded to him.

She wondered if he was going to demand to know why she had led him on and then fled. She had behaved appallingly, she thought miserably, but he did not look angry, and when his beautiful mouth curved into a slow smile her heart-rate quickened. Last night he had looked stunning in a formal suit, but this morning—in jeans and a cream shirt open at the throat to reveal a glimpse of dark chest hair—he was raw, mascu-line perfection, and she could not take her eyes from him.

'Did you sleep well, Tamsin?' he queried, transferring his smile briefly to the flustered-looking waitress who was pouring his coffee.

He seemed to have a devastating effect on all women, Tamsin noted sourly when the girl knocked over the milk jug and apologised profusely as she mopped up the mess.

'Yes, thank you,'

Bruno seemed unconvinced by her reply. 'Your room here at the hotel is comfortable?' he persisted.

'Yes—it's a bit small, but it's fine.' Perhaps he was hoping to taunt her that she would have been more comfortable sharing his room, not to mention his bed? she thought darkly. She met his gaze and smiled sweetly. 'How about you—did you have a good night?'

'Unfortunately not. I spent a very restless night. But we both know the reason for that, don't we, *bella*?' he said dulcetly, his dark eyes glinting with amusement when she blushed. 'Sexual frustration is not a comfortable bedmate, I find.'

She was surprised that he was teasing her with no sign of anger, and her feeling of guilt doubled. 'I'm sorry about last night. I realise I gave you the impression that I…that I was…'

'That you shared my urgent need to make love?' Bruno suggested, and the way his voice caressed the words 'make love' sent a quiver down Tamsin's spine. 'It is a woman's prerogative to change her mind,' he said lightly, reaching across the table and tilting her chin with one lean, tanned finger when she refused to look at him. 'Patience is not one of my finer virtues. I rushed you, but I understand that you did not feel ready to explore this fiery attraction that burns between us,' he murmured softly.

Tamsin stared at him wordlessly, fascinated by the specks of gold in his dark eyes. Tiger's eyes, she thought, as she dropped her gaze to his mouth and remembered how good it had felt when he had kissed her. She wished he would do it again, and gasped when he traced his thumb over her lower lip in a sensuous caress. She wondered if he knew how badly she wanted him to replace his thumb with his mouth… The sultry gleam in his eyes warned that he did, and it took all her will-power to sit back in her seat.

'I suppose you will be going back to Italy soon?' she said breathlessly. He would return to his billionaire lifestyle and she would never see him again, she accepted, wondering why she felt so ridiculously disappointed when he nodded.

'And now that the wedding is over, I assume you will return to London?'

'Yes, but not immediately. My sister lives just north of here, and I'm going to visit her. But this part of Kent is so beautiful, and I want to visit Hever Castle—I don't know if you've ever been, but the Italian Garden is stunning. And I promised James I'd go to Ditton Hall and discuss his plans for the house.'

'Don't you think he'll be busy?' Bruno demanded shortly. 'I understand several of his relatives are staying at the Hall.'

'Oh, they're leaving today, and Annabel is going to stay with friends in Cornwall,' Tamsin explained cheerfully. 'James will be on his own, and I thought he might like some company.'

Bruno stiffened as anger surged through him. It seemed that Tamsin had not spent the previous night with James Grainger after all, but she was still trying to worm her way into his life. He forced himself to smile, satisfied to see the soft flush of colour that stained her cheeks. She might have set her sights on the wealthy Earl, but she was not as immune to *him* as she would like him to believe.

'I do not know this part of England well, but it is, as you say, very beautiful, and I am intrigued by this Italian Garden. Let's do a deal, Tamsin,' he suggested in his rich, sensuous voice. 'You will show me the castle, and in return I will take you to dinner tonight.'

'But I thought you had to return to Italy?' Tamsin faltered, desperately trying to dampen her excitement at the idea of spending the day with him. After her behaviour last night, she was amazed that he wanted to have anything more to do with her, but his dark eyes were warm and he seemed genuinely eager for her company.

'That was my intention,' he agreed, 'but something has happened to cause me to change my plans—or perhaps I should say someone.'

'I see.' Tamsin strove to sound cool and failed abysmally. The sexual tension that had simmered since he had joined her at the table now blazed between them, and Bruno stared intently into her eyes, as if defying her to deny that she wanted to be with him. He was an inveterate womanizer, and she must be out of her mind to even consider spending five minutes with him, Tamsin thought ruefully. But he was also the most gorgeous man she had ever met, and she couldn't resist him. 'Well, in that case,' she said, 'I'd love to be your guide.'

Hours later, Tamsin flopped onto her bed and stared up at the ceiling, a soft smile on her lips. Bruno filled her mind to the exclusion of anything else, and when she closed her eyes she could picture every detail of his sculpted handsome face. Last night she had been sure of her decision not to sleep with a man she did not know. But after spending all day in his company her certainty and resolve were wavering.

It had been a magical day. Hever Castle, once the home of Anne Boleyn, was a romantic idyll surrounded by a wide moat and magnificent gardens. Bruno had been on a charm offensive from the moment he had assisted her into his low-slung sports car—although he had terrified the life out of her when he had raced along the narrow, winding country lanes at breakneck speed.

'Relax, *bella,* I'm a good driver,' he'd told her with his ir-repressible arrogance, grinning when she clutched the edge of her seat and closed her eyes.

She had no doubt that he was right. He brimmed with self-confidence, and she guessed that he excelled at everything he did. Failure wasn't an option as far as Bruno Di Cesare was concerned. He was a man who always got what he wanted— she just wondered what exactly he wanted from her.

But from the moment he'd tugged her into his arms in a

secluded corner of the rose garden and kissed her she'd forgotten everything but her desire to be with him. He was a witty and amusing companion, fiercely intelligent, and so utterly charismatic that she gradually forgot her natural reserve and chatted to him unselfconsciously.

She was in serious danger of losing her head, not to mention her heart she acknowledged ruefully as she dragged her mind back to the present. She had showered and blowdried her hair, and had wasted the last twenty minutes dithering over her make-up. Fortunately she had packed her faithful little black dress, and teamed with high-heeled sandals it looked elegant and sexy—so at least she had something to wear. The problem of Bruno, and the realisation that she was falling for him, was not so simple to resolve.

She was not in his league, she reminded herself as she checked her reflection in the mirror. He was a billionaire Italian playboy who had absolutely no intention of settling down. Even if by some miracle he decided that he wanted a relationship with her, she did not see how it would be possible when he spent most of his time in Italy, or travelling around the world on various business ventures. She craved the security of a loving relationship, and he was determined to retain his freedom. The idea was hopeless—and yet being with him felt so right. She felt as though she was drawn to him by an invisible thread, that she had known him for ever. But that was ridiculous, she told herself firmly. Four years ago she had believed that Neil was the right man for her, but instead he had broken her heart and severely damaged her self-confidence.

She had arranged to meet Bruno in the bar at seven o'clock, and after glancing at the clock she checked her make-up once more, and on impulse took the diamond necklace that James had given her from its box. She fastened it around her neck. It lifted her dress from elegant to stunning—and, after all, she would not have many opportunities to wear such expensive jewellery.

Bruno was waiting for her when she entered the bar, tall, dark and impossibly handsome, in a dark suit and white silk shirt. He was standing by the open French windows, staring out at the gardens, but swung round as she approached him, an indefinable expression on his face when he first saw her. Something blazed in his eyes—male appreciation mixed with another curious emotion that caused Tamsin to hesitate several feet from him. It was the same look she thought she had glimpsed the previous night, a look of contempt and disgust that caused a trickle of ice to slither down her spine. His gaze seemed to be locked on the diamonds at her throat—but then he smiled and moved towards her, and she told herself that his unsettling expression had been a trick of the light.

'Tamsin, *bella*, you look gorgeous.' In two lithe strides he was at her side, but instead of taking her hand and lifting it to his lips, as he had greeted her before, he slid his arm around her shoulders, lowered his head and claimed her mouth.

Tamsin gasped at the first butterfly-soft brush of his mouth on hers, and he took advantage of her parted lips, his tongue delving between them as he deepened the kiss in a sensual exploration that left her shaken and longing for more.

All day he had been so charming and attentive that he had made her feel like a princess, and now, when he finally lifted his mouth and stared deeply into her eyes, she felt as though she had fallen into the pages of a fairytale and she never wanted to leave.

'I've booked a table at a French restaurant in the village. It's not far to walk, or would you prefer to go by car?' he murmured, glancing at her high heels.

'Oh, we'll walk,' Tamsin replied quickly, shuddering at the thought of travelling anywhere by car with him again.

'Coward.' He grinned.

His eyes crinkled at the corners when he smiled and Tamsin's insides melted. He was so beautiful, she thought dazedly. So funny, sexy, clever— He was everything she looked for in a man, and it was no good reminding herself that she might never see him again after tonight, no good telling herself that it was impossible to fall in love with a man she'd only known for twenty-four hours. Whatever this feeling was—lust, love, she couldn't put a name to it—she just knew that she had never felt this way before. Her body ached for his touch, and she couldn't fight the sexual attraction that shimmered between them.

She knew from the hunger blazing in Bruno's eyes that he wanted her, and she had half expected him to have arranged for them to dine in the privacy of his suite—but it seemed that he was not going to try and bulldoze her into anything, and that made her respect him even more.

The sound of her mobile phone made her start, and she hastily fumbled in her purse to switch it off. 'Oh, it's James,' she said, reading the caller display. 'Do you mind if I answer it?'

'Of course not,' Bruno replied smoothly, but his smile faded the moment Tamsin stepped out onto the terrace to take the call. He had ensured that there had been no time for her to visit Ditton Hall all day, and he intended to keep her mind focused exclusively on him tonight, but it infuriated him that he could not prevent her from having any contact with the Earl.

Tamsin had perfected flirting to an art form, he thought grimly as he watched her laughing and talking animatedly into her mobile. To his intense annoyance he had enjoyed the day with her far more than he had expected. Much to his surprise, she had been an intelligent and interesting companion, and it had struck him halfway through the day that if circumstances had been different his pursuit of her would have been genuine.

But circumstances were *not* different, and beneath her façade of unworldly innocence Tamsin Stewart was a manipulative woman, playing on James's emotional vulnerability. She had to be stopped—and he intended that her undisguised sexual awareness of him would be her downfall.

The restaurant Bruno had chosen was small and intimate, with stone floors and a low-beamed ceiling that added to its rustic charm, but the food was French cuisine at its very best— each course an exquisite temptation that was out of this world.

'Thank you for a wonderful evening,' Tamsin said quietly when they strolled back through the village to the hotel later that night, her hand firmly clasped in his. The long days of mid June meant that dusk was only just falling, and in the soft, fading light Bruno's eyes gleamed with an unspoken invitation that made her heart skip a beat.

'My pleasure, *bella*,' he murmured in his rich velvet voice that caressed her senses. 'Would you like to go back to the bar for a nightcap—or come up to my suite?' He saw the flare of uncertainty mixed with excitement in her eyes, and was confident that she would go with him. All his life he had been able to charm women with the minimum of effort on his part, and Tamsin had proved no exception. She hadn't taken her eyes off him throughout dinner, and he knew from the tremor that shook her body now that she was close to capitulating. To tempt her further, he dipped his head and captured her mouth, heat coursing through his veins when he felt her soft, moist lips part tentatively beneath his as she responded to the kiss with an intensity that inflamed his hunger. It would be no hardship taking her to his bed, he thought caustically. Rarely had duty been so pleasurable.

When Bruno finally broke the kiss, Tamsin swayed slightly, her heart beating so fast that she was sure he must feel it thudding against his chest. She barely knew him, the sensible voice in her head reminded her. But her heart and her body had formed an alliance and did not want to listen. She did not speak—couldn't, because her throat seemed to have closed up—but his gentle smile told her that he understood, and wordlessly he clasped her hand once more and led her into the hotel.

He kissed her again in the lift, a slow, drugging kiss that inflamed her senses, and once they had made the short journey along the corridor, and he had opened the door to his suite, she followed him inside and went willingly into his arms.

She was under no illusion that he was offering anything more than sex, but she couldn't resist him. She believed in love and long-term relationships, and he wanted neither, but something about this man urged her to dismiss her principles and for the first time in her life follow the yearnings of her body.

'Can I get you a drink?'

The rough edge of barely contained sexual hunger in Bruno's tone made Tamsin shiver, but where last night the sound of his voice had brought her crashing back to reality, now it barely impinged on the sensual haze that cocooned her. She did not want to think; it was easier not to. But something that felt this right could surely not be wrong? she thought fiercely. Silently she shook her head, watching him, waiting, and with a low groan he fastened his mouth on hers and initiated a slow, sensual tasting that stirred emotions in her she'd believed were long buried.

Her eyelashes drifted down and she focused on the feel of his warm, firm lips easing hers apart, and the determined thrust of his tongue as he suddenly took the kiss to another level that was flagrantly erotic. It was good—so good that she murmured a protest when he eased the pressure a fraction. 'Don't stop.'

Was that throaty, seductive whisper really her voice? She

was startled to see streaks of dull colour wing along his cheekbones, and felt a quiver of feminine triumph when his eyes
blazed with unconcealed hunger.

'I have no intention of stopping, *cara*,' he growled against
her throat as he swung her into his arms and strode towards
the bedroom.

Tamsin gasped and clung to him, but somehow her fingers
became entangled with his shirt buttons. She freed them one
by one to push the material aside and reveal his broad,
muscular chest—gleaming bronze in the lamplight, and
overlaid with a covering of wiry black hairs that felt abrasive
against her palms.

Bruno set her on her feet and, without lifting his mouth
from hers, found the zip of her dress with unerring fingers and
drew it down her spine. Still kissing her, he slipped the
material over her shoulders and groaned his approval when
he revealed her breasts, barely concealed by her black lacy
bra. Her dress bunched around her waist and he released her
stinging, swollen lips so that he could concentrate on un-
dressing her, tugging the skirt over her hips until the dress
pooled at her feet and she stood before him in her bra and a
tiny black lace thong—and the diamond necklace that had
been a gift from James Grainger.

'Let's get rid of this, shall we?' he said, sliding his hands
beneath her hair to undo the clasp before placing the necklace
on the bedside table. 'I'm sure you don't want to risk
damaging such a valuable trinket,' he remarked silkily, his
heavy lids hiding the flare of distain in his dark eyes.

Bruno's olive-gold skin seemed to be stretched tight over
his prominent cheekbones, giving him a predatory look that
filled Tamsin with a mixture of excitement and trepidation.
She couldn't quite believe she was here, in his bedroom, about
to join him on a very big bed. The thought that he was going

to touch her, caress her, caused her to shiver, and each of her nerve-endings seemed to be acutely sensitive as she waited to feel his hands on her skin.

There was still a small part of her brain that insisted she had taken leave of her senses—and perhaps tomorrow she would regret the moment of madness that had seen her go willingly into his arms. But right now all she could think of was the dull, throbbing ache that started low in her pelvis and radiated out, so that every inch of her body seemed to be clamouring for him to possess her. She had never felt a need like this before. Her sex-life with Neil had been good—or at least she'd believed it had. He had obviously had other ideas. But if she was honest she had enjoyed the cuddling afterwards and the feeling of security as much as the act itself. She didn't want to feel safe or secure with Bruno. She wanted, she realised with a jolt of shock, him to throw her on the bed, spread her legs, and take her with all the primitive hunger she could sense he was struggling to control.

'You are exquisite,' Bruno told her raggedly, and her breath hitched in her throat when he unfastened her bra and tossed it aside, before cupping her breasts in his big, warm palms, rubbing his thumb-pads across her nipples so that they hardened into tight peaks that begged for the possession of his mouth.

Bruno felt a surge of satisfaction at her muffled gasp when he trailed his lips down over the creamy swell of her breast and stroked his tongue back and forth over her nipple. Oh, yes, she liked that—liked it so much that she arched her back so that her dusky pink crests pushed forward provocatively. He moved from one breast to the other, laving each peak in turn until her legs buckled and she clung to him for support.

He could feel her trembling when he hauled her up hard against his thighs and she felt the unmistakable ridge of his erection nudge impatiently between her legs. His plan for a long, unhurried exploration of her body would have to be shelved. His reasons for seducing her suddenly seemed unimportant compared to the hunger that consumed him. He wanted her *now,* with an urgency that shook him as it demolished his self-control. He liked to be in control, always, but he was so turned on that if he didn't act fast he seriously doubted they would even make it onto the bed.

With a muttered oath he lifted her and deposited her on the plush bedspread. There was no time to even pull back the sheets. He needed to be inside her *now,* to bury his shaft deep and feel her muscles close around him. Jaw rigid with tension, he stripped out of his clothes and watched her pupils dilate as he stepped out of his boxers and revealed the full length of his throbbing penis. He glimpsed her faint apprehension and forced himself to slow the pace, exerting an iron will over his eager, hungry body as he stretched out on the bed beside her and leaned over to take her mouth in a deep, sensual caress.

Tamsin kissed him back, her panic receding when she realised that Bruno was in no hurry, and intended to arouse her fully before he expected her to accommodate the awesome length of his manhood, which had sent the breath rushing from her lungs when she'd first seen him naked. His hands were stroking her breasts again, rolling her nipples between his thumb and forefinger until the pleasure was unbearable, and she twisted her hips restlessly, needing him to assuage the ache that was dominating her mind and body.

She felt him tug her lacy thong down her legs before he parted her thighs with a firm intent that increased her excitement. There was no going back now. His fingers were already threading through the triangle of blonde curls and stroking insistently up and down, before pushing gently between her velvet folds to find the slick, wet heat that told him she was ready for him.

Caught up in the swirling mist of sexual anticipation, Tamsin barely registered the noise at first. But it sounded again—louder, infiltrating her mind—until she realised that someone was knocking on the door of Bruno's suite.

'Bruno.' With an effort she tore her mouth from his and pushed against his shoulders. For a few seconds he seemed determined to ignore the noise, and when she denied him her mouth he moved lower, trailing his lips down her throat to the hollow between her breasts.

'It's nothing *bella*. Probably just Room Service or something,' he muttered. 'Forget it and concentrate on me,' he demanded, with a flash of the supreme arrogance that was so much a part of him.

But the knocking sounded again, and with a savage curse he rolled away from her and reached for his trousers. 'Stay there and don't move. I'll be two seconds,' he promised, his eyes blazing as he stared down at her naked body stretched out on the bed.

He disappeared into the sitting room, and seconds later she heard him open the door of his suite. The muffled sound of voices was barely audible in the bedroom, but the interruption had brought with it doubt and uncertainty—and given Tamsin crucial time to think while her heated flesh quickly cooled.

What was she doing? Shivering, she sat up and stared into the dressing table mirror. The reflection showed a woman she did not recognize—a temptress with dishevelled blonde hair falling around her shoulders and cherry-stained, swollen lips. The woman's eyes were glazed and heavy-lidded, but desire was rapidly draining, and now the eyes that stared back at her were wide and troubled.

This woman wasn't *her*, Tamsin thought, shock jolting through her. What had happened to her deeply held belief that sex and love were inextricably linked? Or her vow that she would only give her body to the man she loved? She could not love a man she barely knew. And even though she felt drawn to Bruno in a way she did not understand, that was not love—it was lust.

He was going to hate her, she acknowledged despairingly as she scrambled off the bed and into her clothes. This morning he had seemed to understand her reasons for rejecting him the previous night, but this was so much worse. Only minutes ago she had matched his passion touch for touch, kiss for kiss, and he fully expected to come back to bed and find her ready and eager for his full possession. But she couldn't do it. She didn't love him, and he certainly didn't love her, and although her body longed for him to possess her, she knew in her heart that a few moments of pleasure were not worth the sacrifice of her self-respect.

The voices from the sitting room had faded; presumably whoever had been knocking on Bruno's door had gone, so why hadn't he come back to the bedroom? Perhaps he had decided to fix himself a drink? There was no way she could avoid him, Tamsin acknowledged, her heart lurching at the thought of his understandable fury when she told him she had changed her mind for the second time.

Taking a deep breath, she opened the door and stepped into the sitting room. And stopped dead as her stunned gaze swung from Bruno to James Grainger.

CHAPTER FOUR

'TAMSIN!'

James seemed as shocked by Tamsin's appearance as she was to see him sitting comfortably on the sofa, leafing through a sheaf of documents.

'Hello, James.' She forced the reply, although embarrassment seemed to have robbed her of her voice.

But if she felt embarrassed, James clearly felt ten times worse. His eyes skittered away from her and the view of Bruno's bedroom, and the rumpled bed beyond the door, and he jumped to his feet, the back of his neck brick-red as he bent to collect his papers.

'Right, of course—bad timing, obviously,' he mumbled in his cultured aristocratic accent. 'My apologies to both of you. Bruno, you should have said something when I arrived. I know we arranged to meet tonight, but I quite understand that…other things—' he stared down at the floor, as if wishing a hole would appear at his feet '—take precedence.'

'The fault is entirely mine,' Bruno replied smoothly, not glancing in Tamsin's direction. 'Tamsin and I had dinner together tonight and—well…' He shrugged his shoulders laconically and smiled at James, seemingly unabashed. 'One thing led to another, and I completely forgot we'd arranged to meet. Perhaps we can reschedule for tomorrow?'

'Absolutely.' James practically sprinted over to the door. 'I'll wait to hear from you, Bruno. Goodnight, Tamsin,' he called in a strangled voice over his shoulder, before he shot into the corridor and Bruno closed the door after him.

In the minutes that followed James's abrupt departure Tamsin did not know where to look—although anywhere but at Bruno seemed good. It was ridiculous to feel so embarrassed, she told herself sternly. But only last night James had gently warned her that Bruno was a notorious womanizer, and instead of heeding that warning she had acted completely out of character and been prepared to sleep with him barely twenty-four hours after she'd met him. If James had not interrupted them she would have made love with Bruno—would probably *still* be making love with him, she acknowledged. A tremor ran through her when she looked at him, and her body reacted instantly to the fierce tug of sexual awareness that still held her in its grip.

'Don't look so stricken, *bella*,' Bruno drawled as he strolled across the room towards her.

Something in his voice sent a prickle of unease through her, and she stared at him, shocked by his harsh expression.

'Who knows? If you please me, I might buy you an even more expensive necklace than the one James gave you.'

'I don't understand.' Tamsin shivered. How could she ever have thought his eyes warm? They were as black as midnight, cold and pitiless, and the contempt in their depths was definitely not a figment of her imagination. 'What has my necklace got to do with anything?' She shook her head slowly, trying to collate the thoughts swirling in her brain. 'You *knew* James would come to your suite tonight—you'd arranged a meeting with him.' She paused, trying to understand the message that was hovering at the edge of her mind. 'But then—in the heat of the moment you forgot he was coming?'

Bruno's mouth curved into a parody of a smile. 'I didn't forget,' he told her coolly.

Although that was not quite true, he acknowledged silently. His hunger for Tamsin had been so intense that by the time he had laid her naked body on his bed his only aim had been to assuage his desperate need to possess her. It hadn't been until James had knocked on the door that he had remembered his reason for inviting her to his room, and for a few moments he'd still wanted to forget everything but the exquisite feel of her skin beneath his fingertips, and the sweet, damp heat between her legs that told him she was ready for him.

'But why did you ask James to come tonight when you'd already invited me to dinner?' Tamsin persisted in a shaken voice.

Her eyes were huge in her pale face, but the vulnerable, little-girl-lost-look was all part of her act, Bruno told himself darkly.

'It's quite simple,' he said in a bored tone, crossing to the bar and sloshing a liberal amount of whisky into a glass. 'Do you want a drink?'

'No!'

He shrugged and tipped half the contents of the glass down his throat. 'I set you up, *bella*. I invited you to my room with the deliberate intention of seducing you, knowing that at some point James would turn up and find us together.' He moved towards her and trailed his forefinger down to the vee between her breasts. The delicate floral fragrance of her skin teased his senses, and he realised that his heart was slamming painfully in his chest. 'I have to say you made it very easy for me,' he taunted softly.

'I see.' Something was very wrong. Nausea rolled over Tamsin, and she jerked away from him as if his touch defiled her. 'Do you want to tell me why you would do such a thing?'

'I wanted to end your involvement with James,' Bruno stated bluntly. 'He may be temporarily blinded by your not inconsiderable charms and your pseudo-sympathy, but he's a shy, conservative man, and now that he thinks we're sleeping together he'll forget any romantic ideas he may have had about you.'

'What romantic ideas?' Tamsin demanded in a stunned voice. 'James and I are friends. He doesn't see me in…that way.' She shook her head in angry disbelief as Bruno's words slowly made sense. 'He's the same age as my father, and he's still grieving for his dead wife.'

'Yes—James is lonely and unhappy. What an ideal time for an attractive, *sympathetic* young woman to engineer a relationship with him,' Bruno drawled softly.

'I don't believe this. What sort of a relationship do you think I hoped to *engineer* with him?'

'I think you saw the benefits that could come from having an affair with a rich, older man,' Bruno said, in a hard, cold voice that sounded the death knell to the stupid fantasies she had woven in her head throughout the day. 'You saw that James craves companionship. His daughters are growing up and moving away, and soon he will be alone in his great ancestral home. Perhaps you even saw yourself as the next Lady Grainger,' he continued in that same icy tone. 'And if you grew bored with being tied to a man forty years older than you, a divorce could be extremely profitable.'

He gave a harsh laugh, remembering his stepmother's unforgivable treatment of his father once she had secured his ring on her finger. Miranda was a greedy, conniving cow, and he was certain that Tamsin had been cast from the same mould. 'Meeting a lonely widower who also happens to be a hugely wealthy landowner must have been like finding gold at the end of the rainbow,' he murmured, his lip curling contemptuously.

For a moment the room actually swayed beneath Tamsin's feet, and she gripped the doorframe to steady herself. 'I don't believe this,' she said again, her voice shaking with emotion. 'My relationship—my *friendship* with James is completely innocent. He doesn't have romantic feelings for me, and I have certainly never tried to encourage anything like that.'

'So why does he regularly travel to London to see you? He told Annabel his visits are business-related, but he stepped down from his position as chief executive at the Grainger's store when Lorna first became ill. He has no reason to make trips to the city every Friday—apart from to meet you for lunch. Was it during one of those meetings that you persuaded him to buy you the diamond necklace?' he queried scathingly.

'I didn't persuade him to buy me anything.' Tamsin defended herself furiously, but she could not deny that she *did* meet James on Fridays, and she crossed her arms defensively in front of her.

On one occasion they'd had lunch at a restaurant near to the hospital and for once had had quite a bit to drink—Dutch courage, James had said a shade grimly—before his appointment with the consultant who'd had the results of his tests. But once his cancer had been confirmed he had started an immediate course of chemotherapy that made him feel too sick to eat.

For a few seconds she contemplated telling Bruno the real reason for James's visits to London. Bruno was his friend. Would it be wrong to tell him the truth—as long as he swore to keep the news from Davina and Annabel? But it was not her secret to tell. James was adamant that he did not want anyone to know about his illness—perhaps because he wanted to come to terms with it privately. She had promised James she would say nothing, and she could not betray his trust.

Bruno was watching her intently. 'Nothing to say, *bella*?' he queried silkily.

'My meetings with James are none of your business,' she muttered, feeling a pain like a knife being inserted between her ribs when Bruno's mouth curled in disgust. 'But obviously there were occasions when James wanted to discuss Davina and Hugo's flat.'

'Annabel said the flat was finished weeks ago.'

Annabel said... Suddenly a lot of things made sense—in a twisted sort of way, Tamsin thought numbly. James's younger daughter was a spoilt and self-obsessed young woman, but surely she couldn't really believe that her father was involved with his interior designer?

'What concerns me more,' Bruno continued, 'is that James has invested a considerable amount of money in Spectrum Development and Design—against the advice of his accountant. I understand that your brother's company was close to bankruptcy, and I assume you persuaded James to bail him out. It doesn't sound like the wise sort of business decision I'd expect from James,' Bruno added harshly.

His own father had been revered for his sharp business brain, but his obsession with Miranda had made him careless, and he had been blind to the sharks circling ever closer until the House of Di Cesare had been on the verge of collapse. He would not allow James to follow the same destructive path.

Tamsin was staring at him with wide, stunned eyes. 'What money?' she demanded shakily. 'I don't know about any investment, and I've certainly never asked James to put money into Spectrum. The company *isn't* facing bankruptcy. Daniel would have told me,' she said desperately, when Bruno gave her a scathing look.

'Two months ago the bank was ready to retract its support unless Spectrum repaid its debts,' Bruno said coldly. 'Curiously enough, the figure owed matched the amount of James's investment.'

'But I didn't know anything about it—' Tamsin broke off, her mind whirling. Spectrum was Daniel's company, and she was simply one of his employees. But he was also her brother—he wouldn't have kept something as serious as the threat of bankruptcy from her, would he? she wondered sickly. And how had James become involved?

She stared at Bruno and saw the contempt etched onto his hard features. It was clear that he really believed she was money-hungry and had latched onto James, and the realisation made her want to crawl away and hide.

Another thought struck her. 'You say that James is your friend—but if you really believe he has developed romantic feelings for me, why did you arrange for him to find us together? Didn't you think he might be upset?'

'Sometimes it is necessary to be cruel to be kind,' Bruno informed her, with such haughty arrogance that Tamsin forgot her misery and trembled with rage. 'I felt it was better for James to realise what kind of woman you are now than to be disillusioned later.'

'And what kind of woman am I?' she whispered, her throat hurting as if she had swallowed glass.

'A gold-digger,' Bruno replied flatly. 'Before you knew who I was, you couldn't even be bothered to look at me. But the moment you learned I was a billionaire you abandoned James and fell into my arms. I'm not sure what last night was about,' he went on relentlessly, ignoring her muffled gasp at his decimation of her character, 'but I imagine it was to whet my appetite and inflame my desire for you.'

He moved suddenly, taking her by surprise as he snaked his arm around her waist, gripping her chin with his other hand to tilt her face to his. 'I have to admit, your tactics were successful,' he said, in a low voice that throbbed with a mixture of sexual hunger and self-disgust. 'I still want you, Tamsin, and although I'm sure you'll deny it, you want me too.'

He slid his hand down to her breast, and to her abject shame Tamsin felt her body betray her. The memory of how he had stroked her naked breasts and laved each sensitive crest with his tongue tormented her, but the cynical expression in his eyes ripped her emotions to shreds.

'So today,' she whispered, her voice barely audible, 'you deliberately set out to charm me?' She remembered how they had walked hand in hand through the gardens of Hever Castle, talking, laughing, enjoying each other's company—or so she had believed. It had been a magical day, one that she knew she would never forget, but now she wanted to weep with mortification as she recalled how she had trusted him and believed that he was as drawn to her as she was to him. 'And dinner tonight? That was all part of your grand plan to win my trust and entice me to your room? You made love to me—' her voice cracked '—simply to end my so called "relationship" with James?'

Bruno stared at her white face. She was good, he acknowledged, feeling some indefinable emotion twist in his gut when he caught the shimmer of tears in her eyes. She looked shattered. But no doubt that was because he had wrecked her plans to ingratiate herself with her wealthy Earl, not because he had genuinely hurt her. His stepmother had been an accomplished actress too, with an inexhaustible supply of tears that had fooled his father every time.

But tears did nothing for him, and his eyes narrowed as he stared down at the outline of her full, rounded breasts, clearly visible beneath the clingy material of her dress. The first part of his plan had been accomplished. Now that James believed he and Tamsin were lovers, the older man would step back and realise that his future did not lie with the beautiful blonde. But Tamsin did not have to lose out completely, and neither did he

With slow deliberation he began to stroke her breast, gently brushing his thumb across its centre, and heat surged through him when he felt her nipple harden beneath his touch.

'Don't!' Appalled as much by her body's treacherous response to him as his damnable arrogance, Tamsin gasped and tried to draw away, but he felt the tremor that ran through her body and laughed.

'Why not, *bella*? You know we're good together,' he taunted softly. 'Half an hour ago you could not disguise your desire for me any more than I can deny my hunger to possess you. Forget James,' he urged, his voice suddenly fierce and feral with sexual tension. 'I can give you what you want.'

Before she could think of a reply to his arrogant statement, he swooped and claimed her mouth in a searing kiss—hot, hard, forcing her head back as he thrust his tongue between her lips. The chemistry between them was a potent force she could not deny. Her body remembered his touch and trembled with renewed desire, but her pride fought a desperate battle and she tore her mouth from his, breathing as if she had run a marathon as she pushed against his chest.

'How can you want me? You think I'm a…a gold-digger capable of duping a vulnerable man,' she cried wildly.

'True, but I am not a vulnerable man, *bella*—far from it. I know what you are, and to be frank I don't care. I want you naked and willing in my bed. As I am sure you are aware,' he added mockingly, as he slid his hand to her bottom and pulled her up against his hard, aroused body. 'I want you now Tamsin—in the same way that you want me.'

The gleam in his eyes, coupled with the note of supreme confidence in his voice that said she would be unable to resist him, compounded Tamsin's humiliation, and she shuddered and gagged on the corrosive bile that filled her throat.

'Get your hands off me,' she hissed, and a strength she hadn't known she possessed empowered her to thrust him away from her. 'I would rather die than share your bed.' She sped across the room, terrified that he would come after her—terrified that if he touched her, her body would betray her once more.

But when she reached the door she could not help but turn her head to look at him, absorbing his masculine beauty for one last time. How had she not noticed the inherent cruelty in the curve of his lips, or the hard, unforgiving coldness of his eyes? She had seen what she wanted to see, she thought bitterly. Once again her judgement had failed her. She had married a man who had had no intention of remaining faithful to her, and now she had been drawn to another who had let her believe he was genuinely interested in her while secretly planning to humiliate her.

She had to get away from him before she gave him the pleasure of seeing her fall apart, but she forced herself to speak. 'James told me that you are an honourable man,' she said with quiet dignity as she opened the door. 'But clearly he was wrong. I hope and pray that you rot in hell Bruno Di Cesare,' she added fiercely, her voice shaking with emotion. 'Because that's where you belong.'

CHAPTER FIVE

TAMSIN arrived back at her North London flat late on Thursday evening, and was immediately greeted by her flatmate Jess.

'I was expecting you back from your sister's two days ago,' Jess said cheerfully as she padded into the kitchen in her pyjamas and filled the kettle. 'I was beginning to think you'd eloped with a handsome stranger.' She took one look at Tamsin's shuttered expression and sighed. 'But you're here, so obviously not.'

'Obviously.' Tamsin dropped her case and gathered up the pile of letters from the kitchen worktop. 'Vicky wasn't feeling well, so I took a few more days off work.'

'Oh, dear—what's wrong with her? Nothing serious, I hope.'

'She's pregnant,' Tamsin said, in a voice carefully devoid of all emotion, 'and this time round she's suffering from terrible morning sickness. I stayed on so that I could take the twins to nursery in the mornings and give Vicky a break.'

She felt Jess's eyes on her and sighed. Her best friend had an uncanny knack of reading her mind, but right now Tamsin didn't want to share her thoughts with anyone—or discuss the events of the previous weekend. Within twenty minutes of fleeing from Bruno's room she had flung her belongings in her case, checked out of the hotel and raced out to her car, hurtling along the winding country lanes as fast as he had done earlier that day. Less than an hour later she had arrived at her sister's house and invented an excuse about an uncomfortable hotel bed as she'd apologised for turning up on Vicky's doorstep at midnight.

'Well, that's brilliant news,' Jess murmured, glancing speculatively at Tamsin's pale face and the purple smudges beneath her eyes. 'But I suppose a little part of you wishes it was you expecting a baby?'

'Tricky—unless I've developed the ability to reproduce without any help from a man,' Tamsin drawled. She didn't want to go there, or dwell on the hateful feeling of envy that had speared her when Vicky had announced her news. She loved both her sisters to bits and adored her little nephews and niece, but Jess was right. She *had* wished that she was happily married to a devoted husband, with a baby on the way.

'So how was the wedding reception?'

'Okay.' Tamsin made a show of reading the gas bill, and her voice was deliberately non-committal, but Jess wasn't fooled.

'Just okay, hmm?' she mused. 'You didn't meet any gorgeous men—or even one particular gorgeous man? Like the one who called here on Tuesday night?'

'What man?' Tamsin dropped the letters, her expression so haunted that Jess instantly dismissed the idea of teasing her friend.

'Tall, dark, handsome—if you'll forgive the cliché,' Jess said quietly. 'Italian, I think. He didn't give his name, but he left this.' She withdrew the diamond necklace from her dressing gown pocket and dropped it into Tamsin's hand. 'He said he was sure you wouldn't want to lose it. Oh, and he left a business card.' She took a small card from the kitchen drawer. 'He wrote a message on it, and I've been very good and haven't read it.' She made a vain attempt at humour, but her smile quickly faded. 'Tamsin, what's happened? Who is he?'

'He's no one.' The necklace felt cold and hard in Tamsin's palm. Almost as cold as the lump of ice around her heart. She glanced at the business card and despised herself for the way even the sight of Bruno's name caused a fluttering feeling in her stomach. His message was brief.

> *You know we could be good together* bella. *I promise you will find me a generous lover. Call me.*

The word *generous* made Tamsin want to scream. She could visualise him scrawling the message, could picture the haughty arrogance on his face and his confident, cynical smile that once she had finished sulking she would jump at the chance of an affair with a billionaire. How could she have been so *stupid*, so *trusting,* and so criminally *naïve* as to think he had actually fallen for her?

Ignoring Jess's bemused expression, she tore the card in half and repeated the action again and again, before dropping the pieces into the bin. 'He doesn't exist,' she told Jess coolly. 'Have you made that tea yet?'

The London traffic was teeming, and despite his chauffeur knowing all the short cuts, Bruno's car was making slow progress back to his hotel. He had spent the day with his legal team, working on a takeover bid for one of the House of Di Cesare's rivals, and negotiations had been tense. Usually he relished the cut and thrust of business, the tactics and manoeuvres of boardroom warfare, and the sense of satisfaction when he emerged the victor. But today, for some reason, his mind had not been as focused as usual, and several times throughout the day he had checked his messages on his mobile, annoyance mingling with faint disbelief that Tamsin Stewart hadn't rung.

Of course he expected her to. Not immediately—he'd allowed for a couple of days while she raged and sulked before she accepted that James Grainger was not going to be her sugar-daddy. And then she would read his message again and realise that a virile billionaire was not such a bad exchange for an elderly millionaire. Assuming that she was like all the other women Bruno had known, her finger would dial his number faster than you could say diamond necklace— but not yet, it seemed. She was cleverer than he'd thought.

The memory of the way she had rejected him on the night of the wedding reception taunted him and his jaw hardened. But she was not that clever, and she was in danger of over-playing her hand. He was returning to Italy next week, and he had no intention of phoning her before he left.

If he wanted female company there were several women he could have phoned who would immediately have accepted an invitation to dinner. But he chose to dine alone and spent the evening working. It was past eleven p.m. when he switched off his laptop and phoned James Grainger's London residence—out of curiosity rather than any expectation of talking to the Earl. Annabel had said her father regularly spent Friday nights in town, after his meetings with Tamsin, but he already knew that Tamsin was away—visiting relatives, her flatmate had explained—so presumably James had remained at Ditton Hall.

The phone rang five or six times, and Bruno was about to cut the call when a breathless female voice answered.

'Hello—can I help you? Who's calling, please?'

Tamsin waited impatiently for the caller to reply. It was probably a sales call, and she was tempted to slam down the receiver. Unsolicited calls were annoying enough during the day, but it was late at night, and if she hadn't still been here James would have struggled out of bed to answer it.

'Miss Stewart—what a surprise,' a familiar accented voice drawled sarcastically. 'Although perhaps I should not be surprised by your tenacity, *bella*. James is a very wealthy man.'

'Bruno.' Tamsin's heart leapt into her throat, and to her disgust her hands shook and she had to grip the phone. 'Um…I suppose you want to talk to James—but he's in bed, and I'd rather not disturb him.'

'Have you worn him out, then, *bella*? Spare me the details, please.'

The hateful mockery in Bruno's voice ignited Tamsin's anger, and she coiled the telephone cord around her fingers and briefly imagined wrapping it around his neck.

'You are disgusting,' she hissed. 'The only reason I haven't told James about your despicable treatment of me and your foul accusations is because I know it would upset him.' And James had enough to deal with right now.

'Really? I thought it was because you're worried he might realise the truth.'

'The truth being that I'm a greedy gold-digger, I take it?' Tamsin said coolly, while her insides boiled. 'James is tired because we've had a busy day. I'll ask him to return your call tomorrow.'

Bruno's eyes narrowed at the dismissive note in her voice. He wasn't used to being dismissed—especially by a hoity-toity English miss whom he had good evidence to prove was a conniving bitch. He couldn't believe she was with James, and white-hot anger jabbed his gut as he closed his mind to the image of her in James's bed.

'I'm intrigued, *bella*,' he murmured. 'A busy day doing what, exactly?'

Tamsin thought of the hours she had spent with James in the

hospital. He had needed blood tests, some of his notes had gone astray, and they'd had a long wait in the oncology unit before he'd received the cocktail of drugs that were fighting his cancer. He had been sick on the way home; fortunately his chauffeur, Hargreaves, had managed to pull over in time, and once back at his flat he had gone straight to bed, dismissing her plea that he really must tell Davina and Annabel about his illness with the assertion that he was determined to fight it on his own.

'We went window shopping,' she lied to Bruno. 'James is thinking about redecorating Ditton Hall, and we looked at fabrics and things, putting some ideas together.'

Bruno gave a harsh laugh that grated in her ear. 'And I suppose your next step will be to suggest staying at Ditton Hall while you draw up plans for its renovation? You think you're clever, Tamsin,' he grated in a low, cold tone that sent ice slithering down her spine. 'But I warn you, I'm one step ahead of you, and I will do everything in my power to prevent you from hooking your claws into James.'

Tamsin urgently tried to contact her brother over the weekend, but he was away fishing, and her calls to his mobile went unanswered. She spent most of Monday at one of her project sites, chivvying contractors who had fallen behind schedule and trying to track down a consignment of silk wallpaper that had disappeared seemingly from the planet, and her temper was at boiling point when she finally marched into the offices of Spectrum Development and Design.

'Why didn't you tell me about Spectrum's financial problems?' she launched an attack on her brother the moment she saw him. 'I had a right to know. You asked me to join the company,' she said angrily, 'and you were the one who said you wanted to involve me in the decision making.'

'I do,' Daniel muttered, tapping the end of his pen on the desk and not quite meeting her gaze. 'But I didn't want to worry you. Moving from an established, successful design company like Carter and Coults to Spectrum was a big leap of faith for you. How could I tell you six months after you'd joined me that I'd mucked up big-time? I should have known that turning the house in Mountfield Square into flats would go over budget, but I couldn't foresee that the rise in interest rates would deaden the housing market so that the flats didn't sell.'

'But we were close to *bankruptcy!*' Tamsin cried. 'Don't you think I would have noticed when the administrators moved in?'

'It wasn't as bad as that,' Daniel insisted.

'No, because James Grainger bailed us out.' Tamsin felt the familiar sickness in the pit of her stomach that had been with her since she'd learned that Bruno had been right. James's investment in Spectrum *had* saved it from collapse, and it was little wonder that Bruno was suspicious of her friendship with the wealthy Earl. 'I wish you'd told me,' she muttered miserably.

'One of the reasons I didn't was because James thought you might feel awkward,' Daniel explained. 'I admit that I used your friendship with him…'

'Oh, Daniel!'

'…when I approached him and asked him to put money into the company. But I didn't really expect him to agree—and I made it clear that I didn't. To my surprise he was really interested. He offered to put up the money to keep the bank happy until the Mountfield flats are sold—and he'll get a good return on his investment now that property prices are picking up again.'

Tamsin's face mirrored her doubts, and Daniel sighed. 'Stop fretting, Tam; everything's going to be fine. We just need a couple more good deals and we'll be in the black again. The interiors side of the company is doing great, thanks to you. Oh, and you're seeing a prospective new client tomorrow. You're meeting him at the Haighton Hotel at twelve, so don't be late. I need you to make a good impression.' He grinned and pushed his over-long hair out of his eyes. 'I'm counting on you, sis.'

With Daniel's words in mind, Tamsin dressed to impress the following day. Her self-confidence had been crushed by her divorce, and for many months afterwards she had dressed with the sole aim of fading into the background. But gradually, with Jess's badgering, she had begun to take a renewed interest in the way she looked.

Interior design was about making a statement, and she accepted that clients would judge her appearance while they debated hiring her to design their homes. A bold red and white patterned skirt, a crisp white jacket and matching accessories certainly made a statement, and as she ran up the steps of the Haighton Hotel and glimpsed her reflection in the glass doors, the heavy cloud that had sat over her since her last conversation with Bruno lifted a little.

Why should she care about his opinion of her? She knew she wasn't a gold-digger with her eye on James's fortune—and so, more importantly, did James. Bruno was bitter and cynical—although she couldn't understand why, when he appeared to have everything life and money had to offer. But he was gone—back to Italy, or jetting around the globe—and with luck she would never see him again.

At the reception desk she gave her name, and explained that she had a meeting with Alistair Collins. The clerk made a brief phone call, and a few moments later a pleasant-faced, fair-haired man walked across the foyer to greet her.

'Miss Stewart—it's a pleasure to meet you.' He shook her hand briefly as she returned his greeting. 'If you would like to come up to the suite? I think we'll be more comfortable than in the guest lounge.'

Alistair Collins smiled as he ushered her over to the lift, and after a brief hesitation Tamsin stepped inside and they were whisked up to the top floor. The Haighton was one of London's top hotels, and its décor of muted shades and plush pale carpets exuded discreet elegance. Her client led the way along the corridor to the Ambassador Suite, and she glanced around, admiring the gracious, airy sitting room with its huge windows that allowed sunlight to spill into the room.

A figure was silhouetted against the light. His height and the width of his shoulders were impressive, but it was the arrogant tilt of his head that triggered Tamsin's unease. She glanced questioningly at Alistair Collins, and frowned when he indicated that she should step further into the room while he retreated to the door.

'Miss Stewart's here, Bruno. Will there be anything else?'

'No. *Grazie*, Alistair.'

Bruno swung round to face her at the same time as Tamsin heard the snick of the door, indicating that Alistair Collins had left the room. For a few seconds her muscles froze, and her brain seemed to have deserted her, but her eyes locked on Bruno and greedily drank in the perfection of his face: the planes and hollows formed by his sharp cheekbones, the heavy brows and strong nose, the hair the exact colour of a raven's wing that gleamed blue-black in the sunlight, and the cruel beauty of his sensual mouth.

Her first thought, when her brain reconnected, was that once again her hopes had been raised and dashed by this man. She had come today expecting to discuss a possible commission, and although Daniel hadn't said as much, she knew how important any new business venture was to Spectrum's ailing finances. She had no idea why Bruno had gone to such lengths to bring her here; she just wanted to leave—*pronto*.

Bruno was watching her, his dark eyes trailing over her

in a lazy appraisal that ignited her temper and sent fire surging through her veins. Suddenly it was imperative that she spoke first.

'It was rather juvenile to trick me into coming here, don't you think?' she said coolly, lifting her chin and meeting his gaze steadily, although her heart was jerking painfully beneath her ribs. 'I'm sure your staff have better things to do with their time—as I do with mine.' She turned on her heels and headed for the door. 'I'll see myself out.'

'Sit down, Tamsin.' The command was softly spoken, but it was a command nevertheless, and she turned her head and glared at him.

'Why?'

'Because I haven't given you my permission to leave,' he drawled, still in that quiet, controlled voice that disturbed her more than if he had shouted.

'I don't need your permission, Bruno.'

His smile slashed his face, but it did not reach his eyes, Tamsin noted when he moved away from the window and strolled towards her. 'I expect all my employees to carry out my requests without argument.'

'Then I consider myself fortunate that I am not one of them.'

Nervous, but determined not to be cowed, Bruno acknowledged, feeling the faintest hint of admiration for her. His eyes raked her slender figure, noting how her slim-fitting skirt hugged her hips and the cut of her jacket emphasised her tiny waist, while the top button was at a point that revealed a tempting but decorous amount of cleavage. Power-dressing, smart and yet undeniably sexy—but she hadn't known she was meeting him, and had dressed to please another man. Rage fired inside him, surprising him with its intensity, and the temptation to claim her sassy scarlet-glossed lips with his mouth and kiss her into submission was so strong that his muscles clenched.

'Since I have decided to employ your services, *bella*, you are under my control—so sit while we discuss my requirements.'

The gleam in his eyes was unmistakable: raw sexual hunger that made Tamsin tremble with a mixture of outrage and excitement that she tried desperately to deny. In what way did he want her services—and what exactly were his requirements? The connotation in his words sickened her—did he expect her to be his *whore?*

His mouth twitched with amusement as he read her mind, and Tamsin tightened her grip on her laptop case and held it in front of her like a shield.

'I'd sooner work for the devil than you.'

'Try my patience much more, and you'll find him infinitely preferable.' Bruno swung away from her, sat down on a sofa and indicated that she should join him.

Something about his expression warned Tamsin that the only way she could retain any dignity was to comply and, taking a deep breath, she walked over to the sofa and perched as far away from him as possible.

'This is my villa in Tuscany.'

She glanced down at the coffee table and saw several photographs strewn across it.

'It is in the heart of the Chianti region, about an hour's drive from Florence. The house was built in the seventeenth century and has been in my family for many years, but since my father died ten years ago it has fallen into a state of disrepair. Extensive structural work is now complete, and I wish to concentrate on the interior decoration so that I can use the villa as a weekend retreat.'

Bruno sat back and surveyed her coolly. 'That's where you come in. It's an enormous project, but one that your brother assures me you are capable of. In our preliminary discussions he agreed that in order to devote all your attention to the Villa Rosala you will have to relocate to Italy until the work is complete.'

Relocate to Italy—with him! Tamsin shuddered and tore her gaze from the temptation of his wide, sensual mouth. She would rather relocate to the bowels of the earth. A number of responses came to her mind, but she opted for the most succinct.

'You must be joking.'

His hard stare filled her with trepidation. 'I assure you I'm not. And the amount I'm prepared to pay for your expertise isn't a joke either.' He paused, and then added silkily, 'At least your brother does not seem to think so. In fact I gained the impression when I spoke to him yesterday that he's desperate to win this commission.'

'When you spoke to him…' Tamsin felt as though a net was closing around her, trapping her. 'I assume you somehow persuaded Daniel to withhold your identity?' she said bitterly.

'I simply suggested that it would be good if you saw the photos of my villa without any preconceived ideas.'

Tiny beads of sweat formed on Tamsin's upper lip as desperation edged closer. She hated him. There was no doubt about that when she had spent every night for the past week cringing with mortification at the way she had melted in his arms, unaware that he had set out to deliberately seduce her. But although her mind was strong, her body was playing traitor, and she was agonisingly aware of him. The subtle musk of his cologne filled her senses, and the memory of his bronzed, naked, muscle-packed body taunted her subconscious.

'Spectrum employs two other interior designers besides me. Both are highly qualified, and respected for their flair and innovation. I'm sure they would jump at the chance of *relocating* to Tuscany,' she added, her voice as dry as a desert.

'But I want you, Tamsin.'

The words hung in the air. Since the moment she had

stepped into the room and faced him sexual tension had simmered between them. Now the atmosphere altered subtly, and Tamsin could hear her blood thundering in her ears as her breathing quickened.

'No.'

She moved swiftly, but not fast enough. He caught hold of her shoulder as she jerked to her feet and hauled her back down onto his thighs. His hand moved to her nape, tugged her head back, and for a split second she stared into his eyes, shocked by the raw hunger in their depths, before he lowered his head and captured her mouth in a fierce, possessive kiss.

She fought him furiously. Her pride demanded that she keep her lips tightly closed, and every muscle in her body locked in rejection, but he did not seem to care. His tongue probed with wicked intent, insisting that she open her mouth to him, while his hand moved upwards and his clever fingers dealt with the pins that secured her chignon. Her hair tumbled onto her shoulders, soft as silk, and his low groan of approval quivered with such feral, sensual need that she could not fight him any more.

Sensing her capitulation, he altered the tenure of the kiss, deepened it, and thrust his tongue deep into her mouth to explore her with an eroticism that drove everything but her desire for him from her mind. Her hands, which had been bunched into fists on his shoulders, uncurled and drifted around his neck, but as she buried her fingers in his thick black hair he lifted his mouth from hers, set her back from him, and with cool deliberation gripped her arms and forced them into her lap.

'Can I take it that you will offer no further objections to accepting my commission?'

The mockery in his eyes seared her, and with a low cry she scrambled to her feet, snatched up her case and flew over to the door. 'I wouldn't work for you if you paid me a million pounds. I know what all this is about,' she threw at him, her voice shaking with anger and shame that once again she had been unable to resist him. 'The commission to design your villa is just a ploy to keep me away from James.'

'It's certainly one reason,' Bruno said coldly, violent anger surging through him when he recalled that she had been at James's flat late on Friday night. Had she stayed all night? The idea filled him with revulsion, and another emotion that made him question his true motivation for wanting to end her relationship with his old friend. Surely it wasn't jealousy that burned in his gut? 'I am utterly determined to stop you making a fool of James,' he warned. 'But I have studied the portfolio of your work on your website, and although your morals are questionable, your talent is not. You are a gifted designer and I genuinely admire your work. My private jet will take us to Italy on Friday,' he informed her, his hard stare daring her to argue.

It was obvious to Tamsin he had chosen the day deliberately, aware that she usually met James on Fridays. Of course he did not know that James had received his last course of chemotherapy for a few weeks.

'A car will come for you at ten.'

He opened the door, indicating that their meeting was over, but Tamsin wasn't finished. She hadn't even started.

'Forget it,' she snapped, eyes flashing fire. 'You can't make me go to Italy with you.'

'I agree that I can't physically bundle you aboard my plane,' Bruno conceded with a mocking smile. 'But I'm confident I can persuade you. The simple truth is that you need me, *bella*. Think about it,' he continued silkily, when she appeared to be struck dumb at his arrogance. 'This commission is a fantastic opportunity for your career, and for Spectrum. I am the billionaire head of a globally successful fashion empire. I could call on the world's top designers to decorate my house, but I've chosen you.'

He paused for a moment to allow his words to sink in, and then added, 'I have already told Daniel that I'm willing to allow Spectrum to use my name on future advertising. This commission could raise Spectrum from being a small company to a major player in the world of interior design, and your brother knows it.'

Bruno's eyes narrowed as he watched Tamsin's tongue dart out to moisten her lips. He fought the urge to taste her again, to kiss her until she was soft and pliant in his arms and he could do what he had wanted to do from the moment he had first seen her at Davina's wedding reception—take her to his bed.

'I can't force you to work for me, Tamsin,' he drawled, 'but who would believe that you refused the chance of a lifetime? I would only have to make the odd comment at a party to start the rumours flying. Word would get around that I was disappointed with your ideas and decided not to employ you—hardly the endorsement your brother is hoping for. I fear that would be the end of Spectrum,' he taunted in his soft, mocking voice. 'So, unless you want that to happen, I suggest you are ready and waiting at ten o'clock on Friday.'

CHAPTER SIX

BRUNO'S plane touched down in Florence early on Friday afternoon. Apart from enquiring if Tamsin was comfortable, he had ignored her for the entire flight, his laptop open in front of him and his mobile phone clamped to his ear. But once they were whisked through Customs and had climbed into his waiting limousine, he seemed to visibly relax.

'Home,' he murmured in a satisfied tone, as he sat back and stretched his arm along the seat. 'I have travelled all around the globe, but for me Florence is the most beautiful city in the world. Have you visited here before, Tamsin?'

'I've been to Italy, but not Florence—I spent my honeymoon in Rome. It was beautiful,' Tamsin said quietly, a faint, wistful note in her voice.

She'd been so happy, she remembered sadly, and so in love. She had believed that those two wonderful weeks with Neil were a prelude to the rest of their lives. But her marriage had ended in heartbreak less than a year later, and the memories were forever tainted with the knowledge that her husband had never had any intention of remaining faithful to her.

What a trusting fool she had been, she brooded, as she glanced at Bruno's stern profile. He turned his head, and his eyes were hard and dismissive as he flicked them briefly over her. The perfect symmetry of his features could have been chiselled by one of the Old Masters, and although she told herself that she hated him, her heart lurched as she absorbed his masculine beauty. She obviously had a fatal attraction to heartless bastards, but she would not be foolish again. Bruno stirred her in a way no man had ever done, but she was determined to fight her awareness of him.

She had known from the minute she had walked into Daniel's office and seen his eager, hopeful expression that she had no choice but to agree to accept Bruno's commission. Her brother had put his heart and soul into creating his company, and she couldn't offer a valid reason why she should turn down a deal that—in his words—would put Spectrum on the map.

But although Bruno had forced her to come to Italy with him, she was determined that their relationship would be on a professional level only—and fortunately he must have decided the same thing. The desire that had burned in his eyes a few days ago had disappeared, and when he looked at her now his expression was one of cool contempt.

The roads through Florence were busy, but eventually the car drew up outside a gracious apartment building beside the River Arno and Bruno ushered her inside.

'I have to attend a meeting this afternoon, so we'll drive on to the villa this evening,' he explained, while Tamsin glanced curiously around his home.

The elegant lounge was huge, with a high ceiling and pale walls. Full-length curtains framed windows that looked down on the river and commanded a wonderful view of the Ponte Vecchio. Bruno's tastes were eclectic and expensive—the artwork on the walls were original pieces by modern artists and Old Masters, and the furnishings comprised beautiful silk covered sofas in neutral shades, dotted with brightly coloured cushions.

'This is stunning,' she murmured.

He gave her a cool smile. '*Grazie*. I would like to recreate the feeling of light and space at the Villa Rosala—but, as you will see later, there is much work to do.' He glanced at his watch and walked over to the door. 'I will be at my office for the rest of the day. If you wish to go shopping, one of my bodyguards, Tomasso, will escort you.'

'I don't need a bodyguard,' Tamsin objected. The only thing that had lifted her spirits for the past few days was the thought of exploring Florence's rich cultural history. But she preferred to do so alone, not with one of the henchmen whose brooding presence in the front of the car that had brought them from the airport had put her off trying to talk to Bruno.

'Nevertheless, Tomasso will remain with you at all times. While you are working for me, your safety is my responsibility,' Bruno told her in a tone that brooked further argument, before he swung on his heels and strode out of the door.

It was stupid to wish that he really cared about her, Tamsin told herself later, as she strolled through the busy city streets, the stocky, unsmiling Tomasso at her side. It was more likely that Bruno believed she was a shoplifter, as well as a gold-digger who preyed on rich elderly men, and that was why he had insisted that the bodyguard should accompany her.

But sunshine and blue skies made it hard to feel miserable for long. Florence's history and rich culture as the birthplace of the Renaissance meant that it was a popular place for tourists, and the hour she queued for entry to the Galleria dell'Accademia was worth it when she finally stood before Michelangelo's *David* and felt over-awed by its beauty. The Uffizi Gallery was equally stunning, and to her surprise Tomasso proved to be a charming and knowledgeable guide, who was clearly pleased by her admiration of his city and was eager to show her as much as possible.

Dusk was falling by the time they returned to Bruno's apartment. Tamsin was hot and tired, but happy after an enjoyable day. Tomasso spoke little English, and she spoke no Italian, but they had communicated in sign language and gestures, and they were both laughing as they staggered through the door. Their smiles quickly faded when a grim-faced Bruno strode out to meet them. He grated something in Italian to Tomasso, who flushed uncomfortably and left without another glance at Tamsin, and her heart sank when he turned and glowered at her.

'It appears that no man between the ages of sixteen and sixty-five is safe from you, *bella*,' he drawled sardonically, 'but I would be grateful if you could restrain yourself from flirting with members of my staff.'

'I wasn't flirting with him. I was just being friendly,' Tamsin defended herself hotly, her cheeks flaming when Bruno's brows arched upwards.

'As *friendly* as you are with James Grainger?'

'Oh, for heaven's sake!' Tamsin's happiness instantly dissolved, and her shoulders slumped dejectedly.

She was an accomplished performer, Bruno thought darkly, hardening his heart when he caught the glimmer of tears in her eyes. She knew just how to pull the right strings. She'd spent one afternoon with Tomasso and already he was eating out of her hand—and it was easy to see why, Bruno conceded irritably. In a lemon-yellow skirt and white sleeveless blouse, she looked young and innocent—and at the same time incredibly sexy. Her hair was caught up in a loose knot on top of her head, but stray tendrils curled around her face, and his fingers itched to release her hairclip and bury his face in the silky golden strands.

While Tamsin had been out enjoying herself with his bodyguard he had spent several hours in a strategy meeting with his board. To his furious disbelief he had struggled to concentrate on what was being said because he had found himself thinking about her, rather than ways to increase company profits in the Far East. His usually sharp and decisive mind had deserted him, and as his senior staff had seemed surprised at his inattention he'd been incredulous. Business was his top priority—always—and he'd been shocked by his impatience to end the meeting and spend the rest of the day with a woman he despised, but who intrigued him more than any woman had ever done.

Muttering a savage imprecation beneath his breath, he tore his gaze from the temptation of her mouth, hovered briefly on the firm swell of her breasts outlined beneath her thin top, and jerked away from her, his nostrils flaring as he sought to bring his hormones under control. It was no good reminding himself that she was a woman like his stepmother, or that his father had sacrificed his company, the respect of his peers and his relationship with his only son because of his obsession with a woman who had married him for his money. Even knowing those things, he still wanted her.

But there was no chance he would become obsessed with her. He was sure his interest in her was so intense because of her unexpected determination to resist him and the wildfire chemistry that smouldered between them. The sooner he took her to bed the better, he mused. He would be in control, and as with all his affairs the beginning would spell the end. His lovers never held his interest for very long, and he had no expectations that this pale skinned English rose would be any different.

He spared her another glance and saw that she looked tired and fragile, her eyes huge in her pale face. 'There has been a change of plan,' he informed her abruptly. 'It's getting late, so I have decided that we'll stay here tonight and go to the villa tomorrow.' His mouth tightened when she frowned. 'Is there a problem?'

Yes—him! Tamsin thought viciously, still smarting from his accusation that she had been flirting with Tomasso. 'I hoped to go the villa today. The sooner I start work, the sooner I can leave—which I'm sure suits both of us,' she snapped.

Bruno swore succinctly. 'Tell me, *bella,* do you intend to sulk indefinitely because I've wrecked your chance of securing yourself a wealthy sugar-daddy? Or is there a chance you could behave like an adult so that we can establish a reasonable working relationship?

'I never regarded James as a *sugar-daddy.*' Tamsin threw her hands in the air. 'I am not after his money.'

Bruno gave a disbelieving snort. 'I find that hard to believe when you lead such an expensive lifestyle. You drive a new top-of-the-range car, and your designer clothes will not have come cheap. How can you afford to shop in Bond Street on the salary a small company such as Spectrum must pay you? Someone must have been supplementing your income, and my guess is that you encouraged James to buy you those things you craved but were out of your price range,' he accused her scathingly.

'I did not.' Twin spots of colour appeared on Tamsin's cheeks. 'James has never bought me *anything.*'

'What about a diamond necklace worth several thousand pounds?'

'That was different—it was my birthday present.' Tamsin's face burned hotter. 'It didn't really cost thousands, did it?' she faltered. 'I know I should have refused to accept it, but I didn't want to hurt James's feelings.'

'That was most thoughtful of you, *bella.*'

The mockery in Bruno's tone made Tamsin want to hit him. 'I bought my car and my clothes with some money I inherited,' she told him furiously. 'It wasn't a fortune, but it was a sizeable sum. The sensible thing would have been to invest,' she admitted. 'But the last couple of years since my divorce haven't been much fun and when the money came through my family encouraged me to go mad for once—which I did,' she added defiantly, lifting her chin to meet his sceptical gaze. 'I have never asked James for anything, and I certainly didn't appeal to him to put money into Spectrum. My brother told me that James offered to help—but trust you and your horrible, twisted mind to think the worst.'

She blinked hard to banish the angry tears that stung her eyes. Bruno was looking at her as if she was something unpleasant on the bottom of his shoe, and she was angry with herself for caring what he thought of her. But for some stupid reason she *did* care, and she could not drag her gaze from him.

In his black designer suit he looked every inch the powerful, billionaire businessman, but as well as supreme confidence, he exuded a raw sexual magnetism that triggered a response in her she was powerless to control. She hated the effect he had on her—and, even worse, the mocking gleam in his eyes that told her he knew exactly how he made her feel.

'Did something happen in your past to make you so bitter and mistrustful?' she demanded. She guessed that being a billionaire had its downside. Had he fallen in love with a woman and later discovered she had only been interested in his money? It was impossible to imagine the hard, ruthless Bruno she knew in love, but perhaps when he had been younger…?

Bruno was silent for so long that she thought he would not answer, but then he glanced at her, his face shuttered. 'Oh, yes, something happened,' he murmured derisively, and his tone made her blood run cold. He paused, and then continued in a hard tone, 'I grew up at the Villa Rosala—an idyllic childhood, with parents who adored each other as much as they adored their children. When my mother died, at about the same age as Lorna Grainger when she lost her life, my father was devastated. After thirty blissful years of marriage he was lost and lonely, despite the efforts of my sister and I to comfort him. But then he met a young woman.'

Bruno's face hardened, and Tamsin was shocked by the note of undisguised loathing in his voice.

'Miranda was an actress, with a complete lack of talent but a willingness to sleep with anyone who might further her pathetic career. When she met my father she was in her twenties, and he was over sixty with a heart condition. My mother had died less than a year before, and as soon as Miranda learned that my father was the president of the House of Di Cesare she attached herself to him like a leach. They married a few weeks before the first anniversary of my mother's death,' he revealed bitterly, 'and Miranda immediately insisted that they move to a huge house in the city—more in keeping with her position as the wife of a billionaire.'

'So, did you stay on at the Villa Rosala?' Tamsin queried.

'No. I was a young man, in my early twenties, and in my last year at college. My father wanted us all to live as a family.' Bruno gave a harsh laugh. 'I loved him, and I wanted to be with my sister, Jocasta, so I gave in to his pleas and moved to his new house, knowing that it was big enough for me to be able to avoid Miranda most of the time. Unfortunately, she had other ideas.'

His face darkened, and Tamsin shivered at the fury glinting in his eyes. 'What do you mean?'

'I mean that my dear stepmother quickly grew bored with having an invalid husband more than twice her age, and thought that I would provide her with the active sex-life she presumably wasn't getting with my father.' He saw the shocked expression on Tamsin's face, and his mouth curved into another grim smile. 'When I refused to play ball she was furious, and determined to pay me back for rejecting her. She engineered a situation. I can't even remember now the exact reason she made up to lure me to her bedroom—suffice to say that when I arrived she was naked, and flung herself at me just in time for my father to walk in and find me—as he believed—making love to his wife.'

Tamsin could not restrain her shocked cry. 'But he believed you, didn't he? I mean, however bad it looked, your father must have eventually calmed down and listened to you? You were his son.'

Bruno shook his head. 'Unfortunately I underestimated Miranda's acting skills. She gave a performance worthy of an Oscar, insisting that I had pursued her relentlessly and badgered her for sex, culminating in my bursting into her room and trying to take her by force.'

'She accused you of attempting to rape her?'

Tamsin could not disguise the horror in her voice, but Bruno must have misinterpreted the look of disgust on her face, because he grated harshly, 'I didn't touch her.'

He didn't need to defend himself. Tamsin could see the truth stamped on his face. And she knew instinctively that it *was* the truth. He would never attempt to force a woman against her will. Despite the way he had treated her, she was certain that he was an honourable man with a strong protective streak—arranging for his bodyguard to watch over her this afternoon was evidence of that. She also knew without him telling her that he had loved his father and been desperately hurt by his refusal to believe his word over his new wife's.

'So, what happened?' she asked softly.

'My father threw me out and said he hoped never to see me or speak to me again,' Bruno revealed unemotionally. 'And his wish came true. I understand that after a few years he finally came to his senses and realised how conniving Miranda was—helped when he discovered that she had numerous lovers. But by then it was too late. He had lost the respect of his friends and his peers, and the trust of his board. In-fighting and a series of ill-advised business decisions had brought the House of Di Cesare to its knees. I had moved to the US to live with my father's cousin Fabio, and we were building up the household goods side of the company. I heard rumours that my father regretted the past, and his mistrust of me, but he died before we were reconciled.'

'Oh, that's terrible,' Tamsin whispered.

'No, *bella,* that's the destructive power of love,' Bruno told her harshly. 'My father was blinded by his feelings for Miranda and couldn't see that she was a cold-hearted bitch who was only interested in his wallet. If he'd had any sense he'd have just taken her to bed until his fascination for her died. But instead *love* made a fool of him and he sacrificed everything—including his relationship with me.'

With a muttered oath he pushed open the glass doors and strode out onto the balcony, gripping the railings so hard that his skin was in danger of splitting across his knuckles. After a few moments Tamsin followed him and stood hesitantly in the doorway, her eyes drawn to the tense line of his shoulders.

'I vowed on the day he banished me from his life that I would never mistake lust for a deeper emotion,' he grated. 'Love weakens and destroys. I have no intention of allowing it to weaken me.' He suddenly swung round and moved toward her, his hand shooting out to capture her chin between his long, strong fingers. '*This* is the only truth that exists between a man and a woman, *bella mia*—the mutual exchange of sexual pleasure that does not require messy emotions or ridiculous protestations of everlasting love.'

His eyes glittered like polished jet beneath his hooded lids, and his face was shadowed and unreadable as he swiftly lowered his head and claimed her lips in a hard, stinging kiss that sought to dominate.

Shocked at the unexpectedness of his actions, she had no time to think or muster her defences. Every instinct warned her not to respond to him when his mood was so dark and dangerous, but while she fought to keep her lips clamped together her body was already softening, eagerly welcoming the stroke of his hands over her hips and bottom as he hauled her against the solid strength of his thighs. His tongue pushed insistently between her lips, forcing entry, and Tamsin's will-power deserted her. With a low moan she opened her mouth so that he could explore her moist inner warmth with a thoroughness that left her shaking so badly that she was forced to cling to him for support.

Her weakness for him was humiliating, but she couldn't fight him. She curled her arms around his neck, tipping her head back so that he could deepen the kiss and take it to another level that was flagrantly erotic. She felt his fingers tug impatiently at the buttons of her blouse and heard his muttered curse before he simply wrenched the material apart, sending the tiny pearls pinging in all directions. He dragged her lacy bra cup aside with the same barely suppressed savagery, and for a few seconds Tamsin felt cool air on her bare flesh—until he tore his mouth from hers and bent his head lower, stroking his tongue backwards and forwards over her tight nipple and then closing his lips fully around the rosy crest.

Sensation ripped through her, so that she cried out and arched her back, lost to everything but her urgent need for him to continue sucking her while his wickedly clever fingers captured her other nipple and rolled it between his finger and thumb. It was like gorging on a feast after the past weeks when her body had been starved of him. But it couldn't last.

'Much as I despise myself—I want you, Tamsin,' he grated, his voice laced with self-disgust as he tore his mouth from her flesh and stared down at her. 'I watched you with James Grainger and I knew you were a woman like my stepmother. But unfortunately that knowledge does nothing to lessen my hunger for you.'

His words hit her like icy water, and she gasped and tried to draw away from him.

'You want me with the same urgency,' he told her harshly, daring her to deny it. 'But if you're waiting for me to dress it up with fancy words and promises that are impossible to keep, then you'll be waiting a long time—and we're both going to be hellishly frustrated.' He placed his hand back on her breast, but to her surprise he eased her bra back into place and drew the edges of her blouse together, his eyes gleaming in derision at her obvious confusion. 'We both recognised the chemistry that burns between us the moment we met. Why fight it, *bella?* You know we could be good together, but you resent the fact that I'm not fooled by your innocent smile. You'll come to me eventually,' he mocked. 'And you'd better not make me wait too long.'

The softly spoken taunt brought Tamsin to her senses, and she shuddered with shame and self-disgust. 'I'm afraid you'll be waiting for ever,' she told him, her teeth clenched to prevent them from chattering as reaction turned her blood to ice. 'I admit that you push all the right buttons, Bruno—I award you ten out of ten for technique. But I'm not looking for a stud. All I want to do is to be left in peace to get on with the job you've brought me to Italy to do. So do us both a favour and go and relieve your sexual frustrations with someone else.'

CHAPTER SEVEN

FOUR weeks later Tamsin took refuge from the midday sun beneath the shade of the cypress trees and stared out at the view from the rear of the Villa Rosala. The air was still and heavy, and sunlight shimmered on the patchwork of green olive groves and golden wheat fields, while in the distance the dense forest gave way to towering mountains.

Tuscany in the height of summer was simply breathtaking. She had landed a dream job, designing the eight bedrooms and numerous living rooms of a house that she had fallen in love with at first sight—so why did she feel so restless?

It was because Bruno hadn't come this weekend, she acknowledged heavily, hating herself for her weakness where he was concerned. Since he had brought her to Italy he had spent every week in Florence and each weekend at the Villa Rosala, arriving on Friday evenings and leaving again early on Monday morning, and, although she despised herself for admitting it, she looked forward to his visits with increasing eagerness.

Although their conversations were mainly about her designs for the villa, an unspoken truce seemed to have settled between them—which was not a situation she could have envisaged after their explosive confrontation on the balcony of his Florence apartment, when she had vowed that she hated him—and hated herself more for her complete inability to resist him.

During the drive to the villa the following morning she had avoided speaking to him or even looking at him, but once they'd been alone in the big, beautiful old house she'd been unable to ignore the wildfire chemistry that burned between them. She was aware of the undisguised desire in Bruno's eyes, and knew it was mirrored in her own, but a gut instinct for self-protection warned her that she could not give in to the dictates of her body while he held such a low opinion of her morals.

'I swear I have no ulterior motive for my friendship with James, and I wouldn't have allowed him to buy me things even if he'd offered,' she had insisted during Bruno's last visit, when he had made yet more disparaging comments about avaricious women and rich old men.

They had been sitting on the terrace enjoying the late afternoon sunshine, Bruno looking like a bronzed demi-god in cream chinos and shirt, his hair gleaming like black silk and his dark eyes shaded by designer sunglasses. His sinfully sexy body would tempt a saint, Tamsin had thought despairingly, let alone a woman who hadn't had sex for years and whose libido had suddenly stirred into urgent life.

She had searched desperately for a way in which she could prove to Bruno that she wasn't the gold-digger he believed, and once again she had been tempted to tell him about James's illness. But James had entrusted her with his secret and she owed him her loyalty.

'Instead you shopped for designer dresses using money you had been bequeathed in a will?' Bruno drawled silkily.

'That's right.'

'But the story of your inheritance isn't quite so straightforward, is it, *bella*?' he continued. 'You were not left a small fortune by a grandparent or a close relative. For several years you befriended an elderly gentleman—a neighbour who had lived alone since his wife's death and had no other family.'

Tamsin wondered how Bruno knew so much about her, but finally nodded her head in agreement. 'Yes, Edward Abbot— Ted—had been on his own for years. He was a wonderful, fascinating man; he flew Spitfires during the War, and was shot down over France. His arthritis meant that he couldn't walk very well, but he was determined not to go into a care home. I used to get bits of shopping for him, and help him with his housework, although really I think he just liked having company. When he died, I couldn't believe that he had named me as his only beneficiary.'

'No, it must have been a shock—a very pleasant one,' Bruno commented softly, and this time there was no mistaking the mocking note in his voice.

'What is that supposed to mean? What exactly are you suggesting?' Tamsin demanded angrily.

'I was merely pointing out that you seem to make a habit of making friends with wealthy, lonely men.'

The realisation that Bruno believed her friendships with Ted and James were all part of a Machiavellian plot to get her hands on their money made Tamsin feel physically sick, and she swung away from him before he saw her angry, humiliated tears.

'You can't go through life thinking that every woman is like your stepmother,' she snapped.

But of course that was exactly what Bruno had done, since the day his father had remarried and given his loyalty to his new wife rather than his son. Tamsin understood the reasons for Bruno's bitterness, what she didn't understand was why she felt so hurt by his insistence that she was no better than Stefano Di Cesare's second wife.

Bruno had returned to Florence soon after that argument,

speeding down the drive with tyres squealing, throwing up clouds of red dust, indicating his impatience to be gone. The days after he had left had dragged past, and although she hated herself for it Tamsin had counted the hours until Friday evening. But Bruno hadn't arrived then, or over the weekend, and now it was Monday and she had resigned herself to the fact that she would not see him for another week.

Clearly other interests had kept him in Florence, she thought dismally, recalling the image of the stunning dark-haired beauty he had been photographed with in the newspapers. The sight of the woman clinging possessively to his arm had caused a sick feeling in the pit of Tamsin's stomach, which had added to her irritation with herself. Of course he had a mistress, she'd told herself angrily. He was a handsome billionaire playboy and he was hardly going to live like a monk.

Cursing her stupidity, she stretched out on the grass and closed her eyes. She hadn't slept well all week, and had lost her appetite despite the wonderful meals the housekeeper and cook Battista plied her with.

Her emotions were a mess, she conceded disgustedly, and her pride seemed to have deserted her, because despite knowing that Bruno despised her—she could not stop thinking about him, or fantasising about him making love to her.

A dark shape was shading the sun. Tamsin frowned and stirred before she slowly opened her eyes and stared at Bruno's hard profile. He was lying beside her on the grass, propped up on one elbow. Silhouetted against the hazy apricot light, he reminded her of an exquisite sculpture. But when he turned his head towards her she was achingly aware that his golden skin was *not* hewn from marble, and knew that it would feel warm and sensual beneath her fingertips.

Shocked by his unexpected appearance, she could not

disguise the flare of desire in her eyes. The boundaries between dreams and reality blurred. She didn't know if he was real, or a figment of her imagination but it no longer mattered, and she lifted her hand to him in unspoken invitation.

'Do you often cry in your sleep?'

His voice dispelled the lingering cobwebs in her mind and she quickly dropped her hand and sat up. Her cheeks were wet, but when she went to brush her fingers over her face he forestalled her and caught a stray tear with his thumb-pad.

'It's just a dream I have sometimes—it's nothing,' she said shakily. It was months since she'd had that dream, and the fact that it had returned was an indication of her unsettled state of mind. She shifted beneath Bruno's speculative stare, feeling the familiar tug of awareness at the sight of him in faded denims that moulded his thighs and a black tee shirt through which she could see the delineation of his powerful abdominal muscles.

'You were calling for Neil. I heard you from down by the pool,' he said brusquely. 'That was your husband's name, wasn't it? Do you often dream about him?'

Tamsin frowned. 'No, never,' she replied tersely. 'You must have been mistaken. He's the last person I would dream about.' She could not hide the faint bitterness in her voice, and she flushed when Bruno gave her a curious glance.

'Why did you split up? You were only married for a year, I understand. Love's young dream did not last very long, did it?' he murmured mockingly, reminding Tamsin of his scathing opinion of marriage.

Bruno did not believe in love or fidelity. He would never understand the devastation she'd felt when she had learned that Neil had been unfaithful, and she had no intention of confiding in him. 'We realised that we wanted different things,' she said shortly. 'It seemed sensible to end our relationship sooner rather than later.'

Her face was shuttered, but Bruno caught the note of regret in her voice and was irritated by it. She sounded as though she was genuinely sad that her marriage had failed, and he wondered why he disliked the idea that she might still have feelings for her ex-husband. 'I'm sure the sizeable divorce settlement offered some consolation,' he drawled laconically. 'I understand your husband was a wealthy banker?'

Tamsin drew a sharp breath and jumped to her feet. 'I won't even try to dignify that statement with a reply,' she hissed. 'Think what you like, Bruno. I really don't care. Why are you here, anyway?' she snapped. 'I assumed you were busy with your girlfriend.'

'Which one?' Bruno queried lazily, following her across the lawn.

'The one you're pictured with in this morning's newspaper,' Tamsin spat.

She marched back towards the villa, but he easily caught up with her, plainly amused by her simmering anger. 'You mean Donata.'

'Do I?' Even her name was exotic, Tamsin thought miserably. 'I'm afraid I don't have a list of the names of all your lovers.'

'It's a long list, *cara*.' Bruno's sudden, unexpected grin caused her heart to flip, and an emotion that felt horribly like jealousy burned inside her when she noted the wickedly sensual gleam in his eyes 'But actually Donata isn't one of them. She's my second cousin, and the only other great-grandchild of Antonio Di Cesare.'

Tamsin shrugged her shoulders, feigning disinterest, but Bruno continued. 'Actually, I dated two beautiful women last night.'

'Bully for you.'

'It was my sister's birthday, and I always spend it with her. Jocasta was deeply affected by the rift between me and my father.' Bruno's brief spurt of good humour quickly faded and his face darkened. 'She was five years old when my mother died. Her birth had taken my parents by surprise, but she was a very welcome addition to the family. After my mother's death Jocasta clung to me, her big brother, and when my father remarried she needed me more than ever. Miranda did not like children,' he added grimly. 'And when my father banished me he refused to allow Jocasta to see me. We were only reunited after my father died, when I returned to Italy and cared for her for the remainder of her childhood. We remain close, and I took her and our cousin to one of Florence's finest restaurants to celebrate her birthday.'

Bruno fell silent as they crossed the courtyard and entered the villa. From his expression it was clear he was thinking about the past, and his hatred for the woman he blamed for destroying his relationship with his father. Tamsin sighed; Bruno seemed determined to believe she was a woman like his stepmother, and she didn't know how she could convince him otherwise.

'The work on the villa is really coming on,' she said when they stepped into the hall. 'The new terracotta floor tiles are down, and most of the paintwork in the lower floor rooms is finished.' She nodded to the workmen, who were busy applying paint in a subtle shade of gold to the walls of the wide, airy hall. She had established a good relationship with all the contractors and smiled at the men, unaware that their gazes lingered on her long, tanned legs and the way her denim shorts moulded her pert derrière.

But Bruno noticed, and was surprised by the intensity of the urge that made him want to grab the workmen by their necks and boot them out of his house. He did not pay them to leer at his woman, he thought furiously, and snarled at them to get back to work before he followed Tamsin into the lounge, his frown deepening. When the hell had he begun to think of her as *his woman?*

But she soon would be, he decided fiercely. All his attempts to dismiss her from his mind had failed—four weeks of agonising frustration was testament to that, he acknowledged derisively. His only alternative was to face the problem head-on and seduce her into his bed.

He was furious that Tamsin seemed to have some sort of hold over him. Despite her protestations of innocence, he was still convinced that she had deliberately forged a friendship with James Grainger for financial gain, and the realisation that she had previously done the same thing with elderly war hero Edward Abbot reinforced his view that although she had the face of an angel she did not have the heart to match.

But this knowledge made no difference to his hunger for her. Night and day he couldn't stop thinking about her, and he was determined to take steps to control the situation. His father's obsession with an avaricious slut had caused him to make a series of business blunders that had severely damaged the House of Di Cesare—but he was not obsessed with Tamsin, Bruno reassured himself. He simply wanted to take her to bed and expurgate his inconvenient desire for her.

'I've made up a workboard of fabrics and colour schemes for the dining room, but I don't know if you've time to look at it now,' Tamsin said, while Bruno glanced around the sitting room that looked bright and stylish now that the dark walls had been painted in shades of cream and peach. 'Are you going back to Florence tonight or in the morning?'

'I shall be here for the next few days at least. I don't have any meetings scheduled, and I can just as easily work here as at my office.'

'I see.' Tamsin's heart lurched, and she immediately decided that she would avoid him as much as possible. She was terrified that she might unwittingly reveal how much she longed for him to take her in his arms and kiss her. 'Well, I'll do my best not disturb you,' she murmured.

She made to walk past him, but he stepped closer, blocking her path. 'But you do disturb me, Tamsin,' he said softly. 'You've disturbed me since the moment we first met.'

His eyes glittered with unmistakable invitation, but from somewhere Tamsin found the strength of will to fight the insidious warmth that flooded through her veins. 'When you decided that I was planning to con a vulnerable widower out of his money, you mean?' she snapped coldly.

Bruno was too close. She could feel the warmth of his body, and her senses flared when she caught the subtle musk of the cologne he favoured. She needed to move away from him *now*, while she could still think straight, but he reached out and ran a finger lightly over her cheek before cupping her chin in his palm.

'I have been thinking about that,' he murmured, his voice as soft and sensuous as crushed velvet. 'And maybe I was wrong.'

'You don't really believe that,' Tamsin whispered, even while hope flared in her chest. 'You think I'm a woman like your stepmother.'

Bruno had moved closer still, and now his arm snaked around her waist, drawing her body into intimate contact with his. His eyes were hooded and slumberous, but Tamsin could feel his tension, and knew he was exerting his formidable will over his body, to prevent himself from lowering his head and ravishing her mouth with hot, hungry kisses. But she *wanted* him to kiss her, she acknowledged as a tremor ran through her. She wanted it more than she had ever wanted anything in her life.

'I'm not what you think I am. I'm really not,' she told him huskily, her eyes locked with his by some invisible force. 'Now I know about your family history I understand why you assumed the worst of me, but I swear that I have no hidden agenda for my friendship with James.'

She couldn't bear him to think she was unscrupulous, but as his head lowered slowly towards her everything but her frantic need to feel his lips on hers faded from her mind.

The last time he had kissed her, on the balcony of his apartment, he had sought to dominate and punish her. This time he was no less dominant, and his lips were firm as he determinedly parted hers, but the underlying gentleness of the kiss tore down her fragile defences, and she responded to him with all the pent-up need that had been building since she had arrived in Italy.

Bruno slid his hand into Tamsin's hair and angled her head so that he could deepen the kiss. Her mouth felt soft and moist beneath his, and the tentative stroke of her tongue sent blood thundering through his veins.

'You are like a fever in my blood,' he growled. He hated himself for his weakness, but he had fantasised about making love to her for weeks, and now that she was in his arms he couldn't fight the temptation of her silk-soft skin beneath his fingertips. With a muttered oath he caught hold of the hem of her tee shirt and dragged it over her head. She made no attempt to stop him, and when he reached round and unfastened her bra she shivered and stared up at him with undisguised excitement in her eyes.

She gave a little gasp when he cupped her breasts in his hands. He knew what she wanted, and his body hardened and strained uncomfortably against his jeans as he trailed his mouth down her throat and then lower. Her nipples had already swollen to tight, hard peaks, and he laved first one and then the other with his tongue, before closing his mouth around one crest and sucking until she whimpered with pleasure.

'I'm prepared to accept that I may have misjudged you,

bella,' he murmured, as he lifted his mouth from her breast. He moved up to claim her lips once more in a slow, drugging kiss that stoked the fire burning inside him. He frowned, startled to realise that it wasn't just a line to coerce her into his bed. Maybe he *had* been wrong about her? he brooded, his eyes narrowing as he studied the delicate beauty of her face.

But right at this moment he didn't care. The contrast of her pale creamy skin against his darker flesh was an irresistible temptation. He wanted to see and feel her naked body beneath his, and his fingers deftly released the button of her shorts and slid down the zip before he lifted her and laid her down on the sofa.

In his haste to join her he knocked into a low wooden table, scattering Tamsin's design magazines and a pile of postcards over the floor. He had already settled his body on top of her, and he cursed and stretched out an arm to gather up her things, rubbing his hips sinuously between her thighs and thinking of nothing but his urgency to remove the rest of their clothing and sink his aroused shaft deep into her.

'You must have written to half of England,' he muttered as he retrieved several postcards depicting famous sights of Florence.

He threw them onto the table and stared at Tamsin, tempted by her softly swollen lips and her dusky pink nipples that strained provocatively towards him. *Dio,* he was desperate for her—but whilst his body was clamouring for sexual fulfilment his brain had registered something that made him hesitate, and glance again at the postcard on the top of the pile.

'Why are you writing to James?'

'I…' Tamsin licked suddenly dry lips. Her heart was beating in frantic jerks, and her chest rose and fell in time with her swift, shallow breaths. Seconds ago Bruno's eyes had reminded her of warm molasses, but now they were as hard and cold as polished jet. 'It's just a postcard, that's all, telling him about how the villa is coming on, and what the weather is like here. Why shouldn't I write to him?' she demanded angrily, her desire fading to be replaced with fury as Bruno's lip curled contemptuously. 'He's all alone at Ditton Hall while Davina and Annabel are away.'

She also knew that James had been advised by his doctors to rest as much as possible and keep visitors to a minimum during this break from chemotherapy, but she couldn't explain that to Bruno—and from the look of rage on his hard face she doubted he would listen or believe her anyway.

'How annoying for you that you're stuck here in Tuscany, *bella*,' Bruno drawled, in a voice that sent ice slithering down her spine. 'Given the chance, I'm sure you'd hurry straight to Ditton Hall to ease James's loneliness.'

He slid his eyes insolently over Tamsin's breasts. Her nipples were still hard, begging for the possession of his mouth, and when he trailed his finger across one rosy peak he heard her muffled gasp, saw her eyes darken with desire.

'Bruno…don't!' She brought her hands up to cover her breasts and he gave a harsh, unpleasant laugh.

Madre de Dio! How could he be such a fool? When she'd looked at him with her huge blue eyes and given him that shy, innocent smile, he'd actually started to trust her. But she was a clever little actress—like his stepmother—and he was no better than his father. The thought burned in his brain and fury surged through him, made even worse by the knowledge that his anger was mixed with a primitive sexual hunger that he seemed unable to control.

'I could take you here and now, Tamsin, and we both know you wouldn't stop me,' he taunted cruelly. 'I even admit I'm tempted. I'm as frustrated as hell, and it would be so easy to sate my hunger within your delectable body. But I suddenly find I am fastidious,' he hissed, and he rolled off her and stood staring down at her semi-naked body with such searing contempt in his eyes that Tamsin felt sick with humiliation.

'No!' She gave a sharp cry when he snatched up the postcard she had written to James and ripped it in two. 'How dare you? You had no right to do that. This is ridiculous,' she grated, temper giving her the necessary impetus to scramble off the sofa and drag her tee shirt over her head. 'I'll write to who I damn well like. Either that or I'll leave the villa, terminate my contract and go home. You can't *make* me stay here,' she said, faint desperation edging into her voice when Bruno stood, towering over her, his dark eyes mocking her.

'Oh, but I can, *bella*,' he murmured silkily. 'You will remain here until your work on the villa is complete, and after that I'll decide what I'm going to do with you. But you won't be visiting Ditton Hall any time soon,' he promised in a hard voice.

And after awarding her a look of blistering disgust he strode from the room, leaving Tamsin shaking with rage and misery that yet again she had fallen into his arms, only for him to humiliate her.

CHAPTER EIGHT

A STORM was brewing. The night air was hot and heavy and although the air conditioning was working flat out Bruno felt stifled inside the villa.

He couldn't sleep—but what was new about that? he thought bitterly as he strode through the dark garden down to the pool. If he'd learned anything over the past few weeks it was that sexual frustration was not conducive to a restful night.

He had driven back to Florence at the beginning of the week—only hours after he had arrived at the villa—not trusting himself to remain under the same roof as Tamsin without wringing her neck or giving in to the hunger clawing in his gut and carrying her off to his bed. Common sense told him to forget her, get on with his life and, if necessary, sleep with as many women as it took to eject her permanently from his mind.

But to his disgust his common sense seemed to be in short supply—along with his customary needle-sharp business brain and the ruthless ambition that had earned him the respect of his company board members and the fear of his enemies. It had been a hellish week, and his secretary had been unable to disguise her relief when he had sent her home at six o'clock, telling her that he would be spending the weekend at the Villa Rosala should she need to contact him.

Muttering a profanity, he dived into the pool. The water was blessedly cool on his hot skin, and he swam until his muscles ached but were no longer knotted with tension. How could his cool, logical brain accept his initial suspicions about Tamsin and yet his body still crave hers with a carnal, shaming hunger? And how could it be that, despite knowing her for what she was, he missed her company? During their discussions about her designs for the villa he had found her to be intelligent and interesting, and every week he had secretly found himself looking forward to the weekends so that he could spend time with her.

So Tamsin was different from his usual diet of airhead socialites, he conceded, flipping over to float on his back while he stared up at the starless night sky. But she was no different from every other grasping, eye-on-the-main-chance woman who was attracted to his wealth as much as to him. Women like his father's second wife.

Miranda had seen his father coming, he thought bitterly. She'd understood the vulnerability of a grieving widower and ruthlessly exploited his father's loneliness—and he had been flattered by the interest of a beautiful woman so many years his junior, and fallen for her so hard that he'd been blinded to the glaring fact that she was only in love with his bank balance.

Every instinct Bruno possessed warned him that Tamsin was another Miranda. But he would *not* be another Stefano, he vowed. Tension gripped him once more and he began to slice through the water, completing lap after lap as he fought to exorcise her from his mind.

It was hot, stiflingly hot, and Tamsin felt as though she was in a furnace. She could feel the pain building until it seemed to rip through her, tearing at the fragile threads of life within her. With an agonised cry she fought against the sheet that imprisoned her body like a shroud and sat bolt upright, her chest heaving as she opened her eyes and realised that she was in her bedroom at the Villa Rosala.

She had been dreaming. The old, familiar dream that even after all this time was still shockingly real. The human mind was an amazing thing, her GP had explained gently when she'd visited him, convinced that she was going mad. The stomach cramps and the terrible dragging sensations low in her pelvis were as real as they had been when she'd miscarried her baby, but now that she was awake they were fading, whereas on that day the pain had been unendurable.

She didn't want to think about it. Her body had long since healed, but the pain in her heart was still raw, and she certainly couldn't risk lying down and going back to sleep knowing that she would return to the dream, where she was running along endless hospital corridors looking for her baby. Her room felt like an oven, and she felt a sudden desperate need for fresh air. When she crept through the dark, silent house and stepped into the garden the air prickled with static electricity that warned a storm was coming closer. A low rumble of thunder from the distant hills confirmed it, but she couldn't face going back inside.

For the second week in a row, sleep had eluded her for most hours of each night. Even when exhaustion did finally claim her, towards dawn, she was tormented by images of Bruno's hands caressing her, his lips brushing softly against her skin, until she awoke burning up with desperate, shaming, sexual frustration and an overwhelming desire to burst into tears.

She didn't know why she had dreamed about the miscarriage tonight. She was rapidly turning into an emotional wreck, she thought dismally. And it was no good telling herself that the only reason she thought about Bruno constantly was because her body was fixated with his. She had been drawn to him from the moment she'd first met him—had felt that her soul was joined with his by invisible twine—and despite his cruel, scathing contempt of her, she was terrified that she was falling in love with him.

Thunder sounded again, ominously close, and raindrops as big as pennies spattered onto the stone steps that led down to the pool. Clouds obliterated the moon, and the darkness seemed as cloying as a heavy cloak, but a sudden streak of lightning lit up the sky and illuminated a statue of such breathtaking beauty that she stopped dead, unable to tear her eyes from its perfect form.

'Bruno.'

The sudden dark after the lightning blinded her, but seconds later another bolt zigzagged above and threw his naked body into stark relief as he hauled himself out of the pool.

Her brain was struggling to comprehend that he was really here, and not just a figment of her imagination. He hadn't arrived at the villa before she had gone to bed and, recalling his fury with her the last time she had seen him, she'd told herself that he would probably remain in Florence for the weekend.

But he was here, alive and real, and so utterly beautiful that her breath caught in her throat as she moved slowly, as if in a trance, down the steps towards him.

'Go back to bed, Tamsin,' Bruno's voice sounded harsh, slicing through the cloying night air. 'The storm's nearly on us and you shouldn't be out here.'

Tamsin heard his words but did not heed them as she continued down the steps. The lightning had faded, but not before her eyes had glimpsed the rippling muscles of his chest and abdomen and the awesome power of his erection.

Bruno was here, and she needed him. She needed to blot out the pain of losing her baby—a pain that was as raw now as it had been years ago—and she craved the warmth and the strength and the exquisite pleasure only his body could give. She wanted a re-affirmation of life—proof that she could still experience happiness, however fleeting—and without pausing to examine her actions she walked towards him.

The slow patter of lazy raindrops suddenly became a deluge; thunder echoed around them and lightning split the sky in two.

'Tamsin—go.' He was feet from her, and she heard his sharp intake of breath when she lifted the hem of her nightgown and drew it over her head. Her naked body was milky pale against the darkness, but he could see that her breasts were swollen and ripe for him, her nipples jutting provocatively, begging for the stroke of his tongue and the hungry caress of his mouth.

They stood facing each other, so close that electricity seared between them, making the tiny hairs on Tamsin's body stand on end. Close enough to touch, but not touching—not yet. Two people bound by an invisible force as pagan and powerful as the lightning that rent the sky. Nothing existed but the fierce, primal hunger that made them both tremble. Time and place faded and they were simply a man and a woman, naked beneath the heavens, waiting for that finite moment when passion exploded and swept them up in its storm force.

Bruno was breathing hard, his chest heaving as he sought to control the dictates of his body and failed. 'You have one last chance, *bella*,' he ground out roughly. 'If I touch you I won't be able to stop. Not this time.'

'I don't want you to stop.' Tamsin's eyes were slowly growing accustomed to the dark, but although she could not see him clearly her other senses were so acute that she could feel the heat emanating from him, and hear each harsh, jerky breath he took. 'I can't fight you—*this*—any more,' she whispered. The chemistry between them was a potent force she could no longer deny, and she needed him as she needed oxygen to breathe.

His control snapped suddenly, violently. 'Tamsin,' he reached for her like a man in a dream who fully expected her to disappear beneath his touch. He ran his hands up her arms and pushed her wet hair back from her face with fingers that shook slightly. Thunder sounded directly above their heads, a harsh, primitive growl, as he hauled her up against his rain-slicked chest and captured her mouth in a hungry, desperate kiss.

One hand tangled in her hair, holding her fast, while his mouth crushed her lips with an urgent passion that matched hers. It was as if the restraint he had enforced over his body for the past weeks had suddenly burst, and his hunger was a seething torrent that smashed everything in its path. Tamsin clung to his shoulders and matched him kiss for savage, yearning kiss, parting her lips and welcoming the erotic thrust of his tongue. The storm raged around them, but she was conscious of nothing but her clamouring need to feel him deep inside her, for his body to join with hers in a pagan ritual as old as man so that they became one.

'*Dio*, what are you doing to me?' he muttered harshly as he swept her into his arms and laid her down on the sodden grass, immediately covering her body with his own. 'I knew you were a sorceress, *bella*. You make me feel like I'm the strongest, most powerful man in the world, and yet at the same time you weaken me.'

This last accusation was barely audible, and the words seemed to be wrenched from his throat, clawing at Tamsin's heart. She understood him—understood how he must resent this wildfire passion and his shocking level of need, as she did. And yet, like her, he could not fight it.

It was even worse for him, because he despised and mistrusted her, believed she was like the stepmother he hated.

How he must hate himself for his inability to resist the chemistry that bound them together. Tenderness swept over her and she slid her fingers into his hair as he lowered his head to her breast. The rain was falling so hard that it felt like needles piercing her skin, enervating each nerve-ending so that her entire body felt acutely sensitive. She could smell the wet earth mingled with the primitive perfume of male pheromones, and when he drew one pointed, throbbing nipple into his mouth she arched her back and gave a thin, animal cry that was swallowed up by the noise of the storm.

Her body had been created for his touch, she thought when he slid his hand down and pushed her thighs apart, with a rough impatience that made her tremble with anticipation. Despite his urgency she knew instinctively that he would never hurt her, and when he parted her his fingers were gently persuasive, teasing her with butterfly-soft caresses before slipping inside her, one and then two digits, tenderly stretching her in readiness for his full possession.

'Bruno, please—now.'

She dug her nails into his rain-wet shoulders and anchored there as she tried to urge him down onto her. She couldn't wait. Every muscle in her body ached, and she twisted her hips as the subtle movements of his fingers created a spiralling knot of tension low in her pelvis. With shaking hands she pushed his soaking hair back from his brow and caught the feral glitter in his dark eyes as he slowly lowered himself. She could feel the solid ridge of his erection push into the soft flesh of her belly, and then nudge insistently between her legs as she stretched them wide and lifted her hips to welcome him.

The savagery of his first thrust startled her, and her audible gasp caused Bruno to still, his shoulder muscles bunched and his breath shallow and rasping in his throat.

'Tamsin?'

She heard the questioning note in his voice, and as she felt him slowly withdraw she frantically wrapped her arms around his neck, pulling him down so that he gave a muffled groan and thrust again, deep and fierce, as he took her with a primitive force that was shocking and wonderful. Tamsin felt her vaginal muscles close around him, and she smiled a secret smile of feminine triumph when the last vestiges of his control splintered and he drove into her in a pagan rhythm that sent them both spiraling higher and higher towards the edge of heaven.

Her last conscious thought as waves of intense sensation closed over her was that this was where she was meant to be—in his arms, her body joined with his in the most fundamental way.

He was still driving into her with strong, hard strokes, but his pace had increased, become more urgent, and suddenly she was there, her body suspended for timeless seconds, before rapture devoured her and she sobbed his name over and over in the intensity of her climax. As she writhed beneath him, he paused and snatched air into his lungs. She could feel the thunderous beat of his heart echoing in unison with hers, and she opened her eyes to see his face, shadowed and mysterious in the enveloping dark.

A thin sliver of moonlight spilt from behind the clouds and settled on the hollows and planes formed by his sharp cheekbones as he threw his head back and muttered a savage imprecation in his native tongue. She knew he was trying to prolong the moment of release, but then he surged into her one final time, his harsh groan of ecstasy muffled against her lips as he claimed her mouth in a searing kiss. His big body shook, and she wrapped her arms around him and held him close, loving the feel of his weight pushing her into the damp earth.

She could have remained there for ever, beneath the wild night sky while the torrential rain lashed their bodies, but eventually Bruno lifted his head from the hollow at the base of her throat and stared down at her, his expression unfathomable.

'You certainly choose your moments, *bella*,' he growled. Another flash lit up the sky and he rolled off her and tugged her to her feet. 'We'd better get inside before we drown or we're electrocuted—although the lightning is nothing compared to the sexual energy generated between us.'

With her hand imprisoned in his they raced through the rain, back to the house. Tamsin could only imagine what they looked like, naked and so wet that their hair was slicked to their heads, and she prayed that Battista was not awake and watching the storm from the window of the staff cottage.

Bereft of the heat of Bruno's body, her skin quickly chilled, and she was shivering by the time he led her into the master bedroom. The subtle shades of silvery grey and duck-egg-blue worked brilliantly, she mused as she glanced around his room, which was the first in the villa she had completed. The bedside lamps she had chosen to complement the décor looked perfect, but the glow they emitted seemed blinding after the dark, and she blushed when Bruno's dark eyes settled on her.

'You can't be embarrassed now,' he said, plainly amused when she crossed her arms over her breasts. 'Not after what we just shared. Or are you only a wildcat on dark and stormy nights?'

'Don't!' She shuddered at the memory of her wanton response to him, but he caught hold of her wrists and tugged her arms down, naked desire burning in his gaze as he cupped her breasts in his palms.

'You are incredible Tamsin,' he muttered raggedly. 'I have never felt such hunger for a woman, or known such fierce passion. And I am greedy for you again.' The last was uttered on a raw note, as if he was ashamed of his need for her.

Colour winged along his cheekbones as her startled gaze

rested on the jutting length of his arousal. Oh, God—again, and so soon. She was conscious of an answering heat flooding through her veins and pooling between her thighs as he stroked his thumb-pads gently over her nipples. She stared at him wordlessly, hopefully, and with a muttered oath he lifted her into his arms.

'Next time we'll enjoy the comfort of my bed, rather than making love in a mud bath. And, talking of baths…' He shouldered the door to the *en suite* bathroom and carried her into the shower, where he activated the spray and proceeded to soap every inch of her until she was panting and mindless with wanting him.

He shampooed her hair, and when they were both free of all traces of mud, he wrapped her in a towel and rubbed her dry. He took his time, and was clearly amused when her patience snapped and she flung the towel to one side before curving her arms around his neck.

'Now, Bruno—please, *now*.'

Her husky plea shattered his restraint and made a mockery of the idea that he should wait a while before making love to her again, to give her body time to adjust to the power of his possession. Muttering something in his own language, he lifted her and strode back into the bedroom, tumbling them both onto the bed and lifting her so that she straddled his hips.

'Oh, yes—now, *bella*,' he growled, his eyes glinting at her shocked expression when he guided her onto his swollen shaft. 'Have you never done it like this before?'

She flushed at the note of faint surprise in his voice and shook her head, her eyes widening as she absorbed him deep into her, and then gasped when he clasped her hips and began to rock her up and down. It was exquisite, and when she fell forward and he captured first one nipple and then its twin in his mouth she was sure she would die of pleasure. But instead the sensations kept on building as he taught her to ride him. The last of her inhibitions dissolved beneath his murmurs of encouragement, and their mutual climax was so intense that she almost blacked out. It was only the sound of him groaning her name that kept her anchored to consciousness.

She did not know how long she lay on top of him, their bodies still joined, the silence fractured by the sound of their ragged breathing, but at last he rolled her onto her back, stretched out beside her and tucked his hands beneath his head. Without the comfort of his arms holding her close the warmth quickly drained from her body, and doubts and re-criminations assembled in droves. The silence shredded her nerves, and as last she sat up and swung her legs over the side of the bed—only to find herself trapped when he snaked his arm around her waist and hauled her back.

'Don't even think of leaving.' His voice was cool and con-trolled, no hint of the fire that had blazed between them minutes before.

The underlying note of mockery hurt, even though she had mentally prepared herself for it, and Tamsin shivered, her eyes wide and wary when she turned her head to look at him.

'I think we have proved conclusively that, whatever else we might think of each other, neither of us can deny that the passion between us is wilder and more elemental than anything nature cares to dole out,' he said dispassionately. 'From now until the villa is finished you'll spend the nights here with me, *bella mia*, and that's not negotiable—*lo capite*?'

'How can you bear to make love to me, thinking of me as you do?' she asked, shaken by the hardness in his eyes. 'I thought you were too *fastidious*?'

With one swift movement he tugged her down so that she was flat on the mattress and rolled on top of her, trapping her beneath him. He was fully aroused, and Tamsin drew a sharp breath when he slid his hands beneath her bottom, lifted her, and entered her with one powerful thrust that took him deep within her. His eyes locked with hers and his mouth curved into self-derisive smile.

'Clearly not *too* fastidious,' he murmured, and then captured her mouth in a brutal kiss that cut off her angry response and drove everything but the exquisite sensation of his possession from her mind.

When Tamsin opened her eyes next morning it was to the sight of a blue and cloudless sky revealed through the open curtains. The storm of the previous night might have been a dream, but her aching muscles and the feeling of drowsy contentment served as a reminder of her enthralling sex session with Bruno—both in the garden and then throughout the rest of the night that she had spent in his bed.

'*Fool*,' she berated herself as she padded over to the window and stared out at the sun-soaked garden, where scarlet geraniums had already recovered from their battering by the rain and vibrated with exuberant colour.

The pool glinted aquamarine at the far end of the terrace, and the sight of it made her groan as she recalled how she had stripped and offered herself to Bruno like a sacrificial virgin. She was hardly virginal, she thought derisively. Not after a night in which he had seemed intent on expanding her sex education. Caught up in a flaming vortex of passion, she had proved a willing pupil—and she had been tutored by a patient and wickedly inventive master.

She would never be able to look Bruno in the face again, she thought despairingly, covering her hot cheeks with her hands. Where was her pride when she needed it? Buried, along with her self-respect, her brain replied caustically. When she was away from him she could think logically, but the moment he held her and looked at her with that hungry gleam in his eyes she was lost.

He had told her that he wanted her in his bed while she remained working at the villa, and although she should refuse him she knew she would not. He was offering nothing but sex. Even though they had shared the most wondrous, incredible pleasure in each other's arms, his attitude towards her had not softened. He despised her, but he wanted her, and she would not deny him when it would be denying herself too.

She had no idea where he had gone, or whether he expected her to wait for him, but it was a working day, and the minuscule dribble of pride she still retained insisted that she should get on with the job he had brought her to Tuscany to do. As she emerged from his room, clutching his robe around her, she heard his voice floating up the stairs. She guessed from the one-sided conversation that he was speaking on the phone, and her few words of Italian meant that she could not have eavesdropped even if she had wanted to. But something in his tone made her pause on the landing.

He sounded as though he was having an argument with whoever was on the other end of the line. Not a furious row; his short, staccato phrases reminded her of a bickering lover—now angry, now cajoling—as if he was trying to make someone see his point of view.

It was a familiar scenario, she thought grimly, remembering the occasions when she had caught Neil muttering secretively into his mobile phone. His explanation had invariably been that he'd been speaking to someone from the golf club—or work, or the gym. And she'd believed him. In her trusting, Pollyanna optimism that their marriage was working, she'd never doubted her ex-husband's word or his loyalty.

It was only after Neil had gone that she'd realised those calls had been from Jacqueline. Now, as she pushed open her bedroom door and heard Bruno's voice again, this time catching a name, she wondered what was so important that he'd risen early to talk to his beautiful cousin Donata.

CHAPTER NINE

AUGUST slipped lazily into September, and the view from the Villa Rosala became a tapestry of reds and burnished golds as the leaves on the trees turned from green to russet. Tamsin spent the days overseeing the completion of her designs for the house and her nights in Bruno's bed, where their fierce passion showed no sign of fading.

This was possibly the closest place on earth to heaven, she mused one morning, as she stood in the huge, rustic kitchen, looking out at the mist that lay like a silver cloak over the distant fields. Tuscany was impossibly beautiful, and she was falling more deeply in love with each passing day—and not simply with the countryside, the voice in her head warned.

Bruno filled her mind as he filled her body—utterly and completely. She could think of nothing but the exquisite pleasure of his warm skin sliding on hers, and the sound of his gorgeous, sexy accent when he teased her or murmured softly in Italian as they lay together in the afterglow of making love.

If she wasn't careful he might become her reason for living— and that would be a dangerous situation. It was hard to believe that they had been lovers for over a month, but now the villa was very nearly finished, and it was time she went home.

Somehow—incredibly—their relationship had evolved

over the days and weeks from a bitter, resentful passion to something that was softer, occasionally even gentle, and anger had been replaced with tentative friendship. She knew that Bruno still mistrusted her, but he no longer accused her of being like his stepmother. She had even thought briefly of trying to discuss her friendship with James Grainger, but the same problem remained. James had specifically asked her not to tell anyone about his cancer, and she still could not give Bruno a viable reason for her regular meetings with the Earl.

Even if she did break James's trust, and Bruno believed her, he still thought she had deliberately befriended her elderly neighbour and persuaded him to make her a beneficiary in his will. On balance it seemed safer not to upset the fragile peace between them for the short time that she had left at the villa.

Lost in her silent reverie, she jumped at the sound of his voice. 'The bathroom suppliers have just phoned.' Bruno strode into the kitchen and Tamsin spun round, the sight of him in his grey suit and pale blue silk shirt causing a familiar weakness in her lower limbs. 'The taps and other fittings that were delayed are now in stock. I told them you would phone back to arrange delivery.'

'Great,' Tamsin replied, desperately trying to inject enthusiasm into her voice. Completion of the *en suite* bathroom attached to one of the guest bedrooms had been delayed because of a problem with the suppliers, but once the fittings were in place she only had to choose towels and a few accessories to match the apple-green decor and the last room in the villa would be finished. 'Hopefully they'll deliver in the next couple of days, and then I'm all done here,' she said brightly. 'I'd better start packing.'

Bruno stiffened in the act of pouring a glass of fruit juice and frowned. 'I didn't realise you were in such a rush to leave,' he murmured, his eyes narrowing when she carefully avoided his gaze.

'I've been here for over two months,' Tamsin pointed out. 'When I spoke to Daniel last week he wanted to know if the villa was nearly finished as he has another commission lined up for me. It seems I'm quite in demand.' She faltered when Bruno's mouth tightened ominously.

'Why do you sound so surprised, *bella*? You have great talent, and the work you have done on the Villa Rosala exceeds all my expectations.'

'I'm glad you like it.' Why on earth did his words of praise cause tears to fill her eyes? Tamsin thought impatiently as she picked up a teatowel and dried a dish draining on the rack so thoroughly that she was in danger of rubbing off the pattern around the edge.

A tense silence fell while Bruno gulped down the juice and poured himself a cup of strong black coffee. He had woken that morning, as he had every other morning for the past month, feeling energised from a night of incredible sex. He was shocked by Tamsin's reminder that she had been staying at the villa for two months. He could hardly warrant that time had passed so quickly—particularly this last month that they had been sleeping together. Without him being conscious of it, they had settled into a routine of domestic bliss that should have set alarm bells ringing in his head, and the realisation that he was in no hurry to change the situation caused him to frown.

When had he begun to view her as his mistress rather than simply another blonde who was temporarily sharing his bed? he wondered. And why was he so irritated by her seemingly happy acceptance that he would want her to leave as soon as her work on the villa was complete? But what was the alternative?

With an angry shrug of his shoulders he drained his coffee cup and snatched up his briefcase, hardly able to believe that he was contemplating asking her to remain at the villa. There would have to be some sort of timescale, he brooded. And rules would have to be drawn up and fully understood by Tamsin before he could issue such an invitation, so that when he wanted to end the affair he could do so without suffering the annoyance of recriminations or tears.

'We'll talk about it when I get back,' he grated as he moved towards her and dropped a brief, hard kiss on her mouth. Her lips instantly softened and parted, and he could not resist the temptation to deepen the kiss, his body stirring when he felt her tongue slide into his mouth to tangle erotically with his. 'Why don't you stay on a while?' The words had left his lips before he'd had time to consider them, and once again he felt a jolt of shock that he did not want her to leave. Not yet, anyway. 'You must be owed some holiday from Spectrum. Spend it here with me, *bella*.'

The throaty invitation sent a quiver along Tamsin's spine, and she gave a silent groan of despair when her body sprang to urgent life. Only this morning Bruno had teased her that she was insatiable, when she had followed him into the shower, boldly encircled his shaft with her hands and stroked him, until he'd growled something in Italian and lifted her onto him, cupping her bottom while he thrust into her.

'I could take a week's leave, but with this new commission pending I can't stay for ever.'

Bruno forced himself to step away from the temptation of Tamsin's delectable body and tried to dismiss the fantasy of removing her clothes and spreading her beneath him on the enormous kitchen table. 'Who said anything about for ever?' he queried idly. 'You should know by now that I don't do eternity, *cara*, but you can't deny it would be more convenient if you continued to live here for a while. Once you're back in London we won't be able to meet up so often. My diary is pretty full for the next few months, and I can't rearrange my schedule to include overnight stops in London.'

He paused in the doorway and glanced back at her, noting how two months in the Tuscan sun had lightened her hair, so that it swung on her shoulders in a curtain of platinum blonde silk. 'Perhaps you should think about resigning from Spectrum?' he suggested, in a casual tone that masked his surprise as the unbidden words left his lips.

'Resign…? And do what exactly?' Tamsin demanded, confounded by the idea.

'I promise I can think of numerous ways to keep you occupied,' Bruno murmured coolly, seemingly unaware of the storm brewing on the other side of the kitchen.

'But this is my *career* we're talking about. I can't give it up just so that we can have a regular sex-life.' She was still reeling from his implication that he wanted their relationship to continue after she returned to England, and the idea that he wanted her to sacrifice her career so that she could stay with him was simply beyond belief.

Bruno glanced at his watch and gave an impatient shrug. 'So get a job here in Italy. I have a lot of influence in Florence, and I don't doubt I could secure you a position with any design company you choose.'

Twin spots of colour stained Tamsin's cheeks, and she put her hands on her hips to prevent them from seizing one of the heavy copper saucepans hanging from the ceiling beams and hurling it at his head. 'You don't think that my honours university degree in Design and several years' experience would count for much, then?' Her voice rose a notch, and Bruno's expression darkened. 'You're saying that even if I was totally useless companies would still offer me a job if I traded on the fact that I'm sleeping with you? Wow! That makes me feel good,' she hissed sarcastically.

'*Madre de Dio!* It's typical of a woman to make—how do you say?—a mountain out of a molehill,' Bruno growled. 'It was just a suggestion, *bella*. If you want to rush back to England, then go. We'll have to put up with the inconvenience of a long-distance affair and meet when I can allocate you time in my diary,' he added nastily, wondering why he suddenly felt the urge to be so unpleasant.

'Always supposing that the slot is equally convenient in mine,' Tamsin said through gritted teeth. How had she ever thought that his arrogance was an endearing trait?

Bruno's mouth tightened and he dipped his head. 'Of course. But I fear that two busy careers are not conducive to a smooth-running affair.'

Tamsin gave a tight smile. 'Well, instead of expecting me to sacrifice my job, you could always give up yours.'

His astounded expression was almost comical, and he stared at her as if she had suddenly grown another head. 'Don't be ridiculous. I am the president of a billion dollar global business empire. My position as head of the House of Di Cesare is my birthright, and soaring profits are proof that I have earned my place at the top,' he added proudly. 'You are blessed with great artistic flair, but—' He broke off and threw his hands in the air in a typically Latin gesture.

'But I'm just a lowly designer?' Tamsin finished grimly.

'I didn't say that,' Bruno exploded, as the last of his patience evaporated. 'I asked you to live with me. I did not expect the invitation to trigger a third World War.' He had confidently assumed that she would jump at the chance to stay on at the villa. He did not ask women to be his mistress every day of the week, and he wondered if she realised how many of his self-imposed rules he was breaking. 'I have to go. I'm late for a meeting,' he snapped, another glance at his watch revealing that he was going to have to phone his secretary and ask her to delay his meeting with a conglomerate of Japanese businessmen.

The day that had started so well with a wild sex session in the shower was rapidly deteriorating, he thought grimly. And it was all Tamsin's fault. He hated being late—and why the hell had she decided to discuss their future relationship now, when she knew he had to get to work? She trailed into the hall after him, and as he opened the front door he caught a glimpse of undisguised misery in her eyes and felt a curious tightening in his chest.

'We'll continue this discussion tonight,' he promised in a softer voice, but another surge of irritation that she hadn't immediately agreed to stay on at the villa with him prompted him to add, 'May I remind you that *you* instigated this morning's sex session, *cara?* I'm not knocking your eagerness,' he drawled. 'The passion between us has always been mutual, and we're both going to suffer the frustration of the damned if we're living a thousand miles apart.' As if to emphasise the point, he skimmed his hand lazily over her breasts and smiled when her nipples instantly hardened and jutted provocatively beneath her thin cotton shirt. 'Think about it,' he advised, his stinging kiss forcing her angry retort back into her mouth.

And while she was still debating which succinct phrase best expressed her fury, he slid into his car, fired up the engine and sped off down the drive.

Bruno was the most arrogant, egotistical…Tamsin ran out of adjectives as her temper simmered. He had made her sound like some sort of nymphomaniac—but the truth was she couldn't have enough of him, she acknowledged dismally, and the thought of going back to England and only seeing him occasionally was unbearable. But could she really give up her position with Spectrum in order to enjoy a few more weeks, at most, with a man who had always made it clear that he did not want a long-term relationship—especially one with a woman he still believed was a gold-digger?

She watched the contractors' van pull up in the front court-yard and four elderly-looking workmen slowly emerge. They should finish the tiling in the guest bathroom today, and she would not need them again—which was probably a good thing, she mused as she waved to the men. The housekeeper, Battista had told her that one of them—Luigi—was over seventy. They worked well, and were clearly master-crafts-men, but every task took twice as long as Tamsin had allowed for. She couldn't understand why Bruno had dismissed all the younger workmen...

His suggestion that she should give up her job and remain in Tuscany with him tormented her for the rest of the day. He had said they would discuss the future of their affair when he came home that night, and she didn't know what she was going to say to him, but she was reprieved from having to make a decision when he phoned late in the afternoon and ex-plained that problems in the New York office meant that he had to make an unexpected trip across the Atlantic. He was flying out the following morning, and had decided to spend the night at his apartment in Florence.

'I'll be back at the weekend,' he promised, when Tamsin could not hide the disappointment in her voice. 'It's only five nights, *bella*. If you decide to go back to England after the villa is finished we'll spend most of our time apart.'

'It will only be four nights if you come back here tonight,' she pointed out, trying not to sound as though she was des-perate to see him, and failing badly.

Bruno laughed, and the low, sexy rumble curled around her aching heart. 'I wish I could, *bella,* but something's come up. I'll see you soon.'

With a heavy heart Tamsin cut the call and wandered dismally around the empty villa. Every room looked stunning, but she found no pleasure in her finished designs, and the house seemed soulless without Bruno's vibrant presence. She could not bear the thought of sleeping alone in his bed, and spent a restless night back in the room she had occupied when she had first arrived at the Villa Rosala.

Finally, in the hour before dawn, she gave up. Bruno hadn't even gone to the US yet, and she missed him so much that she ached. She was under no illusion that continuing her affair with him would lead to happy-ever-after—and after her failed marriage she wasn't even sure it existed—but she'd settle for happy-right-now. And, having made the decision to remain in Tuscany for as long as he wanted her, she was eager to tell him before he left Florence.

Bruno had told her she could borrow the little car that the groundsman, Guido, used whenever she wanted, and she had often driven to the surrounding villages, but never as far as Florence. The sky was still pearly grey, streaked with pale pink, as she sped away from the villa, and she didn't see another vehicle on the road as it snaked through the countryside. An hour later she reached the outskirts of the city. Fortunately it was still so early that the traffic hadn't built up, and with the aid of her road map she managed to find Bruno's apartment without too much difficulty.

By the time she entered the lift her heart was pounding. She must be mad, she told herself. Bruno would have to leave for the airport soon, and she would only be able to see him for a few minutes. Would he be pleased when he learned of her decision to stay on at the villa as his mistress? Or would he already have had second thoughts? Her stomach clenched. What if he had changed his mind and no longer wanted her?

She had a vivid mental image of how he had lifted her into

his arms and made love to her with raw, primitive passion in the shower the previous morning and her nervousness lessened. He hadn't tired of her yet—and who could say, the little voice of optimism in her head whispered, how long his hunger for her would last?

'Signorina Stewart!' Bruno's butler, looking as smartly dressed as ever, despite the early hour, could not hide his surprise when he opened the door.

'Hello, Salvatore.' Tamsin followed him down the hall, her heart sinking at the oppressive silence of the apartment. 'I hoped to catch Signor Di Cesare before he left.'

The butler shook his head. 'He has already gone to the airport.' His usually impassive features softened slightly at her obvious disappointment. 'Sit down and I will bring you a cup of tea, *signorina.*'

Tamsin gave him a weak smile, but as soon as he had gone she stared bleakly out over the river and felt silly tears sting her eyes. Bruno would be back at the weekend, she tried to console herself. But part of the reason for her mad rush to Florence was because she had wanted to tell him she would stay with him before her nerve failed. They would have to make up for lost time when he returned, she decided firmly, a smile curving her lips as she considered on how five nights of abstinence would sharpen their hunger for each other, and how they would probably spend the entire weekend in bed.

It seemed pointless to linger in the empty apartment, but as she stepped into the hall, on her way to tell Salvatore not to bother with the tea, Bruno's bedroom door opened and a woman emerged.

'*Chi sono voi?* Who are you?' she demanded haughtily, in Italian and then in English.

Tamsin stared at the woman, wondering why she seemed

familiar. And then realisation dawned. She was the woman from the newspaper—Bruno's cousin Donata.

'My name is Tamsin Stewart. I…work for Signor Di Cesare,' she explained quietly.

'Is that so?' Donata's perfectly shaped eyebrows arched upwards.

The newspaper photograph had not done Donata justice, Tamsin conceded, studying the young Italian woman's glossy black hair, which tumbled around her shoulders, and her slanting dark eyes. She was seriously beautiful, and Tamsin felt a flicker of unease when she strolled into the hall, fastening her robe as she moved—but not before Tamsin glimpsed the skimpy black lace negligee she was wearing. It was obvious from her sexily tousled hair and the sleepy yawn she hastily hid behind her hand that she had spent the night in the apartment. But why was she coming out of Bruno's bedroom, looking like a smug sex-kitten who had gorged on cream?

'Tamsin Stewart?' Donata shrugged her shoulders uninterestedly. 'Are you a new maid? I'm sure you weren't here on my last visit. And shouldn't you be wearing a uniform?' she demanded, glancing at Tamsin's colourful cotton skirt and strap top. 'Just because Signor Di Cesare isn't here, it is not an excuse for standards to drop. You can run my bath and then get changed.'

'I'm not a maid. I'm an interior designer and I'm currently working on Bruno's villa.' Tamsin struggled to ignore the woman's rudeness, dredging up a smile that wasn't returned. 'I…need to go over a few things with him regarding some of my designs.' She invented a valid reason to explain her visit.

Donata's eyes had narrowed when Tamsin had used Bruno's Christian name rather than the more formal Signor Di Cesare, and she said mockingly, 'This early in the morning? You're very keen, Miss Stewart.'

Tamsin felt the betraying flare of heat scorch her cheeks, but ploughed on. 'I thought I might catch him before he left for his trip.'

'Well, you're too late. Bruno left twenty minutes ago, and he was running late then. I'm afraid we overslept…' The woman's mouth curved into a coy smile. 'After an energetic night.' She paused, her brilliant gaze noting how the colour leached from Tamsin's face. 'Oh, dear—you're not another of Bruno's little girlfriends, are you? I really must learn to be more discreet.'

Nausea slopped in Tamsin's stomach and made a mockery of her determination to remain calm. 'What do you mean? I know who you are,' she said, more strongly. 'You're Bruno's cousin.'

'Second cousin,' Donata corrected her softly. 'My father and Bruno's father were cousins, and I am a Carerra, but I am Antonio Di Cesare's great-granddaughter, and eventually, of course, I will take the Di Cesare name—when Bruno and I marry.'

'When you marry?' Tamsin parroted. 'Are you saying you are engaged to Bruno?'

Tamsin felt a curious buzzing sensation in her ears and she gripped the edge of the bureau. Years ago, when her ex-husband had admitted he was having an affair, she'd been sure she would never again feel such a raw sense of betrayal. But this was much worse. The idea that Bruno could be planning to marry his stunning olive-skinned cousin, with her knowing eyes and cruel smile, made her feel physically sick.

Donata shook back her silky curls and stretched languorously. 'It's not a formal arrangement at the moment, but there has been an understanding between us for years. I'm not sure if you know anything of Bruno's history,' she continued, glancing speculatively at Tamsin, 'but after his father banished him he moved to the US and stayed with my family. My father, Fabio, has never made any secret that he would love to have Bruno as his son-in-law,' she continued, 'and Bruno is very close to Fabio, so…' She shrugged her shoulders and smiled maliciously at Tamsin. 'I'm not sure Papà would be so pleased if he knew I actually share Bruno's bed on my regular visits to Florence, so we keep that a secret,' she said in a mock whisper, placing one long, scarlet-painted finger-nail across her lips.

Tamsin's stomach twisted, and she shook her head disgustedly. 'It sounds like a marriage made in heaven,' she said tightly. 'But what about love?'

Donata looked at her incredulously, and then threw back her head and laughed. 'What *about* love, Miss Stewart? As far as I'm concerned it's not a vital commodity to a successful marriage, and Bruno shares my view.'

She stepped closer and stared intently into Tamsin's face. 'Don't tell me you've fallen for him? You fool,' she said spitefully. 'Bruno isn't interested in *love*; he saw how it destroyed his father and he vowed when he was a young man that he would never repeat Stefano's mistakes. We're ideally suited, he and I,' she stated confidently. 'We both have something to gain from marrying—for me, money and power, and for Bruno, the strengthening of the Di Cesare bloodline, because I am a direct descendant of Antonio Di Cesare. Much as I loathe the idea of pregnancy, I'm prepared to give Bruno a child. You don't think he'd sacrifice all that for you, do you?'

She saw the confusion in Tamsin's eyes and gave another cold smile. 'Until we formalise our relationship, Bruno is free to indulge his predilection for attractive blondes. You're not the first, Miss Stewart, and I doubt you'll be the last. But ultimately Bruno is mine, and I'm prepared to wait for him for as long as it takes.'

Tamsin was saved from having to try and formulate a reply when the butler appeared, bearing a tray. 'Your tea, *signorina,*' he murmured, his bland features not flickering as he glanced from Tamsin to Donata.

'That won't be necessary, Salvatore. Miss Stewart is just leaving,' Donata said coolly. 'I'll let you show her out.'

She pushed past Tamsin, into the lounge, and Tamsin followed Salvatore dazedly down the hall, feeling as though her legs would give way at any second. When the butler opened the front door, she managed a faint, ironic smile.

'Thanks for the tea, Salvatore.'

He nodded gravely, and his stern expression softened imperceptibly. 'Sometimes situations are not always as they seem, *signorina*. I will inform Signor Di Cesare of your visit.'

'*No!*' Tamsin shook her head wildly. She had a feeling that Donata would not mention her visit to Bruno, and it would be the ultimate humiliation if he should ever find out that she had rushed to the apartment after only one night apart and come face to face with his lover and future wife. 'Please, Salvatore, don't say a word,' she begged, and after several moments' hesitation he slowly nodded and closed the door.

CHAPTER TEN

LONDON in early November was unremittingly grey and wet. The leaden skies were as heavy as Tamsin's spirits, and she shivered when she emerged from the Underground station and was hit by a blast of icy wind.

Christmas was over a month away, but the shop windows had been festooned with festive decorations for weeks, and Oxford Street was teeming with frantic shoppers.

It was a far cry from the hot, still days of summer in Tuscany. The two months she had spent at the Villa Rosala belonged to another time, another world, she thought bleakly. It had been a time of fleeting happiness that she had always known could not last, and it had ended abruptly when she had fled from Bruno's apartment in Florence with his cousin Donata's mocking laughter ringing in her ears.

Back at the Villa Rosala, she had written him a brief note, explaining that she had decided to return to England to continue with her career, and then she'd left and caught the next flight back to London, where she had spent the weeks since in a state of numb misery that had caused her flatmate Jess serious concern.

Bruno hadn't contacted her, and she hadn't expected him to. For him, their relationship had been a brief interlude of amazing sex with a woman he mistrusted. She suspected that he had resented the sizzling sexual chemistry that held them both in its thrall, and although he had asked her to remain at the villa with him for an unspecified time, he had known all along that he was going to marry Donata.

If nothing else, it proved that she had diabolical taste in men, Tamsin conceded with a grim smile. The only difference was that she had been married to Neil, and he must have known that his infidelity would break her heart. Bruno had never made any promises, but the image of him making love to his beautiful, sultry-eyed cousin hurt a hundred times more than when she had read a text message on her ex-husband's phone and realised that his work colleague Jacqueline was also his mistress.

She had returned to England determined to pick up the threads of her life, but as the weeks had passed a new concern had supplanted her misery and caused her to study the calendar with a growing feeling of dread. A home pregnancy test had confirmed her fears, and she had been even more shocked when her GP had sent her for an ultrasound scan to determine her dates, and she'd learned that she was eleven weeks pregnant.

'I can't believe it,' Jess had said, when Tamsin had confided in her. 'I thought pregnancy was supposed to make you put *on* weight, not lose it. You've been fading away since you came back from Italy. I assume it is Bruno's baby?' she'd added darkly. 'What are you going to do?'

'I don't know.' Tamsin had laid her hand on her flat stomach and tried to assimilate the range of emotions swirling inside her. Elation, joy—fear.

She still could not get her head around the fact that she was expecting Bruno's child. He had always been scrupulous about using protection, apart from one time—the night of the storm. Even now the memory of the explosive passion they had shared that night made her blush. Their loving had been as wild and elemental as the lightning that had ripped the sky apart, and in a strange way it seemed fitting that their child had been conceived at the apex of a thunderstorm.

'You're going to tell him, aren't you?' Jess had insisted. 'You can't do this on your own, Tamsin. I mean, I'll help out as much as I can, but you have to consider your financial situation. You won't be able to work when you're caring for a newborn baby, and Bruno is a billionaire, for heaven's sake. It's only right he should support his child.'

A shudder had run through Tamsin at Jess's words. She could just picture Bruno's fury if she went to him demanding money. 'I suppose I'll have to tell him. He has a right to know. But I don't want anything from him,' she told Jess fiercely. 'This is my baby and I'll take care of him—or her.' Her voice had faltered. 'But it's still early days,' she'd said, her throat constricting as the agonising memory of losing her first baby filled her with fear. 'Anything could happen.'

It wouldn't happen again, she tried to reassure herself now. Her miscarriage had been brought on by the stress of discovering that Neil had been cheating on her throughout their marriage. This time she would not allow anything to upset her, or cause her to risk losing another baby.

But the knowledge that she would at some point have to tell Bruno that she was carrying his child hung over her like a heavy cloud, and the sight of his stunningly handsome face smiling from the front cover of a celebrity gossip magazine had been the last straw. The woman in the picture looked as though she was intent on climbing inside his jacket with him, Tamsin had noted sourly. She was an internationally famous model, and as Tamsin had stared at her she recalled Donata's words that she was happy for Bruno to indulge in his predilection for beautiful blondes until they married.

The sooner she told him about the baby, the sooner she could put him out of her mind and her life, she decided, as she turned down a side street close to Hyde Park. She knew from the magazine article that he was currently in London, and now seemed an ideal time. She was absolutely certain he would not want to have anything to do with her or their child, but her heart was racing with nervous apprehension when she walked into the London offices of the House of Di Cesare.

Bruno got up from his desk and strolled over to the window of his office to stare out at the rain-lashed streets. Usually he exerted such supreme control over his life that nothing ever happened to surprise him. He did not like surprises, he conceded, and nothing had prepared him for the news imparted by his secretary that a Miss Tamsin Stewart was waiting in Reception and wanted to see him.

Why had she suddenly reappeared in his life, almost two months after he had returned to the Villa Rosala—his tiredness from a hellish few days evaporating at the anticipation of taking her to bed—and found that she had gone?

His mouth tightened at the memory. He'd read her pithy little note, explaining that she was returning to her job in London and didn't want the distraction of continuing their affair, with a mixture of anger and disbelief. Being dumped was a new experience for him, and he didn't like it.

Not that he was heartbroken, he thought caustically. Since the day his father had believed his stepmother's lies and told him he no longer considered Bruno his son he had built a concrete wall around his heart that he was confident was impenetrable.

He had cynically wondered if Tamsin was playing a game. Perhaps she believed that his unabated desire for her meant that he was actually falling for her? It was certainly no coincidence that she had walked out on him *after* he had asked her to remain in Italy as his mistress. But if she'd hoped that he would chase after her, she had been doomed to be disappointed. He'd missed her—he would admit that much—but he could live quite happily without her, and the only reason he had instructed his secretary to send her into him in five minutes was because he was curious to know what she was playing at now.

His office door opened and his secretary appeared.

'Miss Stewart's here.'

'*Grazie*, Michelle.' He forced himself to remain at the window for several more seconds before he turned and glanced across the room, and he was irritated to find that his heart was beating uncomfortably fast as he stared at Tamsin.

She had lost weight, was his first thought. Her golden tan had faded, and she looked pale and drawn but no less beautiful. Her incredible blue eyes seemed too big for her face, but he dismissed the idea that she looked fragile with a shrug of his shoulders.

'Please sit down.' He indicated a chair and noted that her hands were shaking when she immediately sat and pushed her hair over her shoulders. He wondered why she was nervous, and why he liked the idea that he disturbed her, but his face was impassive as he resumed his seat and studied her coolly across his desk. 'I'm afraid I'm not quite sure why you are here. Is this a social visit?' he murmured.

'No, not really.' Tamsin licked her parched lips and dropped her gaze to the desk in front of her.

She had been mentally preparing for this for days, but the moment she had walked into his office and seen him—tall and dominant and achingly beautiful—her brain had seized up and she could think of nothing but the memory of the wildfire passion they had once shared. She glanced at him fleetingly and then quickly looked away, her heart hammering painfully in her chest.

'There is a reason why I'm here.' She wished he would say something, rather than continue to stare at her dispassionately, and she wondered if his eyes had ever really been warm during the weeks that they had been lovers, or if she had imagined it. There was no easy way to say what she had to say, and in the end she just said it. 'I'm pregnant.'

'Ah.' Bruno leaned back in his chair and put the tips of his fingers together. 'Of course you are. Why didn't I think you would come up with something like this?'

His sardonic smile stirred her temper. 'I haven't come up with anything. I'm simply here to tell you that I am carrying your child,' she snapped. 'And before you say another word, yes, it's yours—no question. Although actually I really don't care if you believe me.'

Tears burned her eyes. His reaction was pretty much as she had expected, so why did she feel as though he had knifed her in the ribs? She remembered her ex-husband's fury less than a year into their marriage, when she had told him she was pregnant—his disbelief followed by his angry accusations that it was her fault and she must have deliberately missed her contraceptive pill. She had been devastated by Neil's reaction, and distraught at his hints that it was still early days and she didn't have to continue with the pregnancy. She wondered if Bruno was about to make the same suggestion, and a cold slab of anger settled in her chest. He might not want their baby but she did, and she would love and protect the fragile life within her.

Bruno stared at her as if he was determined to see inside her head. 'Forgive me for sounding suspicious, *bella*,' he said softly, 'but I understand that you attempted to persuade your husband to stay with you by telling him you were pregnant.

It didn't work then, and I can assure you that if your announcement that you are carrying my child is a ploy to restart our relationship it's not going to work now either.'

It was amazing how much pain the human body could withstand, Tamsin mused, feeling strangely detached from herself. She even managed to give Bruno a cool smile as she stood up. 'Right—I've done my duty and told you,' she said briskly, picking up her handbag and heading for the door. 'Your reaction is entirely as I predicted, Bruno. I knew you would want nothing to do with your child, and that suits me fine…because I really don't want anything to do with you. Goodbye.'

Her hand was on the doorknob. She was actually going to walk out. Bruno's eyes narrowed. Was she playing another game and gambling on him calling her back? Or was she telling the truth about the pregnancy?

'You've had your pregnancy confirmed I assume?' he growled, his tension rising when she opened the door.

She paused fractionally, her foot over the threshold. 'Yes.'

'How far?'

'Twelve weeks.' Tamsin's pride insisted that she should walk through the door and keep on walking, but she could not resist looking at him one last time.

Bruno's black brows were drawn into a slashing frown as he made a mental calculation. 'The night of the storm,' he said harshly. 'But if you've known all this time, why did you leave the villa? And why wait until now to tell me?'

'I didn't know then. I had an unusually light period a couple of weeks after that night and I assumed everything was all right.' She flushed, embarrassed at having to explain the technicalities. 'I only found out a week ago, and I was shocked when the scan showed my pregnancy was so well established. I could have told you the moment I found out, but—' she gave a faint shrug to hide the bolt of pain that shot through her

'—there is a higher risk of miscarriage in the first three months of pregnancy, and I decided to wait until I was sure I had something to tell you.'

Her voice shook, and Bruno glanced at her speculatively. She looked small and vulnerable, and he had to fight the urge to take her in his arms and simply hold her. His shock at her stark announcement was slowly receding, and he was certain now that she wasn't lying. She really was expecting his baby. He stared at her, searching for signs of her pregnancy. Concealed beneath the folds of that thick woollen coat was a tiny spark of humanity—his son or daughter—and he was shocked by the feeling of possessive pride that surged through him

He had assumed that he would one day have children, although he had never visualised actually settling down and spending his life with one woman. He had taken scrupulous care to prevent any of his mistresses claiming that they had conceived his child. He was cynical enough to realise that many women would consider nine months of pregnancy a small price to pay to secure a regular maintenance agreement from a billionaire—certainly enough to employ a full-time nanny to care for the resulting offspring.

The news that Tamsin was pregnant with his child had initially angered him. How could he have been so stupid as to fall into the age-old trap? But honesty forced him admit that it had been *his* mistake. On the night of the storm his hunger for her had been so urgent that he hadn't even thought about contraception. It was ironic that the first and only time he had ever had unprotected sex he had given Tamsin a child, he thought grimly. But, despite what she thought, he had no intention of shirking his duty.

'Don't look so shattered, Bruno.' Her voice mocked him. 'I don't want anything from you—certainly not your money,' she said bitterly. 'I have no expectations that you'll want a relationship with this baby, but there will come a time when our child will ask questions about his or her father, and I won't lie. I'll have to reveal your identity and make up some story… I don't know—that we loved each other but couldn't be together or something. But you have to accept that your child might want to contact you some time in the future.'

'My child will be able to contact me whenever he or she likes,' Bruno grated. 'Because my child will live with me in Italy and will never be in any doubt that I am its father.' He stared down at her with such haughty arrogance that Tamsin shivered with a mixture of confusion and unease. 'You are carrying the Di Cesare heir. I will not allow him to be born illegitimately.'

'What do you mean?' she whispered, unable to tear her eyes from the stark beauty of his chiselled features.

'I mean that for the child's sake I am prepared to marry you.'

Tamsin did not know what kind of reaction Bruno had envisaged at this astounding statement, but from his thunderous frown it was clear he had not expected her to burst into hysterical laughter.

'Do share the joke, *bella*,' he snapped, when she subsided into hiccups and wiped her eyes with fingers that for some reason were trembling. 'Although I can't say I find the future welfare of our child a laughing matter.'

'I'm sorry.' She gulped for air and found that her emotions had see-sawed and she now wanted to cry. 'It's just that there's a certain irony to this situation that you wouldn't understand.' Years ago, when she'd told her husband she was pregnant, he had promptly divorced her. Now she was pregnant by a man who believed her to be an unscrupulous gold-digger and he was *prepared to marry her*. Big deal, she thought furiously.

'It's kind of you to offer, Bruno,' she hissed sarcastically, ignoring his glowering stare, 'but I have no intention of marrying again—ever. And anyway,' she added before he could speak, 'bigamy is illegal.'

'I thought you were divorced—' he began heatedly.

'I am. But you are engaged to your cousin Donata, and you can't marry both of us.'

'Which trashy gossip magazine did you get that from? Some of the rubbish they print is amazing.'

The look of surprised incomprehension on his face was so good she could almost believe it was genuine, Tamsin thought bleakly. But she knew the truth. She had seen Donata coming out of his bedroom at his apartment in Florence—although she would rather die than admit she had gone there herself to tell him she had decided to stay on at the Villa Rosala as his mistress.

'Well—whatever, I still don't want to marry you,' she said coldly. She was standing in the doorway, but when she tried to step into the corridor he gripped her arm and tugged her back into his office.

'Trust me, *bella,* you're not the kind of woman I would have chosen for my wife,' he drawled sardonically, ignoring her outraged gasp. 'But what we want is no longer important. We have a duty towards our child, and it is a duty I intend to fulfil to the best of my abilities.'

'Even if that means marrying a woman you believe is a conniving bitch, like your stepmother was?' Tamsin queried tightly.

Bruno's eyes gleamed like chips of obsidian—hard and cold and utterly remorseless. 'Even then,' he agreed harshly.

For a moment despair threatened to overwhelm Tamsin, and she gripped the doorframe for support. 'You must know it would be a marriage made in hell,' she whispered. 'How could we live together, make a life together, when there is so much mistrust between us?'

'We managed when you were living at the villa. In fact I recall that we had a very successful relationship.'

'We had a lot of sex,' Tamsin snapped, aware from the sudden prickling of her skin that the atmosphere had subtly altered.

From the moment she had stepped into his office an undercurrent of sexual energy had smouldered between them. Since she had fled from Italy she had only felt half alive, but within seconds of seeing him fire had surged through her veins once more, and each of her nerve endings felt acutely sensitive as her body responded blindly to his magnetism.

His eyes were half hidden beneath his heavy lids, but she caught the glint of feral hunger and she stood, paralysed, as he slid his hand into her hair and tugged her head back so that she was held prisoner.

'Sex cannot be the basis of marriage,' she said tremulously, her eyes locked on his mouth as he lowered his head towards her.

He laughed. 'It's a better basis than love,' he taunted. 'Which is such an overrated emotion—don't you think, *bella*?'

'I believe that love is the only reason for two people to get married.'

His mouth was so close to hers that she could feel his warm breath on her lips. She could not respond to him—must not. But her whole body was shaking, and she would surely die if he did not kiss her. She gave a little moan, half-pleasure, half-despair, when he traced the contours of her mouth with his tongue, and she could not help but part her lips in readiness.

'If you are hoping for love, then I'm afraid you're going to be disappointed,' Bruno murmured. 'But think of the consolations—not only do you get an explosive sex-life, but you've managed to catch yourself a billionaire husband after all.'

His mouth cut off her furious retort and he ground his lips on hers, demanding a response her traitorous body was shamefully willing to give. He crushed her to him, and through the thickness of her coat she could feel his hard, aroused body, feel the answering heat pool between her thighs, and she gave a sob of wretched despair. The weeks without him had been hell, and now that she was in his arms once more she accepted that he was her reason for living. But he didn't love her and he never would, and the knowledge was tearing her apart.

From somewhere she found the strength to tear her mouth from his and push against his chest. 'All the riches in the world wouldn't persuade me to marry you,' she choked. 'I won't do it, Bruno, and you can't make me.'

His mouth curved into a smile totally devoid of warmth as he promised, 'You will, *bella*, and I can.'

CHAPTER ELEVEN

'ARE you okay Tamsin? It's not too late to change your mind, you know.'

Tamsin glanced around the packed register office, filled with friends and family, and in every conceivable space vases of flowers, and gave her brother a rueful smile. 'I think it is. Mum would kill me—and you too, for suggesting it. She's fretting enough as it is because the registrar has been held up by the snow.'

Daniel Stewart grinned, but his voice was serious when he said, 'She and Dad wouldn't mind. They're worried you're rushing into this marriage. I mean, they like Bruno, and so do I. He seems a good bloke—not like that last git you married,' he muttered caustically. 'I know Bruno will take care of you and the baby. But you haven't seemed happy since you set the date for the wedding, and we all want you to be sure you're doing the right thing.'

'I am,' Tamsin replied steadily, with no hesitation in her voice to betray the doubts that had plagued her for the last six weeks. She was done with worrying, she decided, her eyes straying across the room to where Bruno—looking stunningly handsome in a dark grey suit and blue silk shirt—was chatting to her father. During the many sleepless nights she'd endured since she had told him she was carrying his child she had fought a bitter battle in her head—unwilling to marry a man who would never love her, but desperate to give her unborn baby a secure and stable upbringing with both its parents. And, inevitably, the needs of her baby came first.

When Bruno had first made his shocking announcement that his child would not be born illegitimate, she had been adamant that she would not marry him. She had wrenched free of his arms and hurtled along the corridor in a frantic bid to escape him. But a sharp pain had made her seek the bathrooms, and the discovery that she was bleeding had sent her stumbling back to him, sheer terror and despair in her eyes as she sobbed that she was losing their baby.

To give Bruno his due, he had taken charge of the situation with the decisive determination of a military chief, lifting her into his arms and carrying her into the lift, then bundling her into the car that was already waiting out front and whisking her off to a private hospital.

The consultant she'd seen had tried to reassure her that occasional spotting in the first few months of pregnancy was not unusual, and that as Tamsin had no more pain everything was probably fine. An ultrasound scan had confirmed that their baby was developing normally, but as memories of her miscarriage had flooded back, Tamsin's tenuous hold on her emotions had given way and she'd wept—as much for the baby she had lost as the one she'd feared she was about to lose.

From that moment on Bruno had taken charge of her life. And, although she despised herself for her weakness, Tamsin had let him. She had not even argued when he'd insisted that she move into the apartment he had recently leased. The doctor had suggested bed-rest for a few days, and Bruno had taken the suggestion so seriously that he'd only allowed her out of bed so that he could carry her to the bathroom.

His concern had had a bittersweet poignancy that had made Tamsin cry still more—because she'd known that it was for their baby rather than her.

Living with him day by day, loving him as she did, had been hell on earth, and she wept each night after he bade her goodnight, burying her face in her pillows to muffle the sound of her crying.

The days leading up to the fifteen-week mark, when she had suffered her first miscarriage, had been the worst of her life. But when the date had passed, and her pregnancy had continued normally, a sense of calm had settled over her, and for the first time she'd begun to look to the future and believe that she might carry this baby full-term.

Their child deserved to grow up in a secure family environment, Bruno had argued stubbornly, when she had once again voiced her doubts that marriage between them could not possibly work. She had never heard him sound so passionate. It had been clear that now he was over his shock Bruno wanted their baby as much as she did, and was utterly determined that his child would not be born out of wedlock.

'Well, if this registrar doesn't hurry up, you may not have the wedding today anyway.' Daniel's voice broke into her thoughts. 'Bruno's looking decidedly tense. Hold up—who's just arrived?' he murmured, glancing over to the door.

But it was not the registrar who had just entered the room, and Tamsin gave a shocked gasp at the sight of a familiar grey-haired figure.

'James!'

For a man who had recently had treatment for a life-threatening disease, James Grainger looked remarkably well, and Tamsin told him so when she flew across the room to greet him.

'You're so tanned—and you've gained a bit of weight, thank goodness. How are you?'

'Pretty good.' James smiled. 'A month on St Lucia with my sister and her husband did me the world of good. I haven't got the all-clear yet, but I've got my fingers crossed,' he told her cheerfully. 'Now, tell me, how did you pin this man down?' he chuckled, and Tamsin quickly turned her head, her heart sinking when she met Bruno's unfathomable gaze. 'Congratulations, Bruno. You couldn't have found yourself a more wonderful, generous-hearted young woman than Tamsin.'

'I agree—I'm a lucky man,' Bruno replied quietly.

Something in his tone made Tamsin glance at him, sure she would see the familiar mockery in his gaze, but instead he looked—she frowned—*shattered,* and for a few seconds the expression in his eyes made her heart stop. But then his lashes fell, and she had the distinct impression that he did not want to meet her gaze. Perhaps he believed she had invited James to their wedding and was angry with her, she thought heavily.

But there was no time to explain that James's appearance today was a complete surprise to her, because one of the officials announced that the registrar had arrived and invited everyone to take a seat.

And suddenly this was it—in a few minutes' time she would be Bruno's wife. The strange trance-like calm that had cocooned her since she had slipped into her cream wool wedding dress and matching coat that morning fractured, and her heart began to jerk painfully beneath her ribcage.

Memories of her marriage to Neil came tumbling back. She had been so full of hope and expectations that day, but a year later her dreams had been cruelly destroyed—and, even worse, she had lost her baby. Now she had no hopes and no expectations, she thought sadly as she took her place next to Bruno. All she had was a deep and abiding love for a man who had made it clear he would never love her in return.

For a few seconds panic threatened to overwhelm her. She

couldn't go through with it. Instinctively she placed her hand
over her stomach. The tiny fluttering sensation beneath her
fingers as the baby moved made her heart leap, and the
tension drained from her body. For her baby's sake she could
do anything.

. The ceremony passed in a blur and her hands were visibly
shaking when Bruno slipped a plain gold band on her finger.
She could not bring herself to look at him, but she could feel
the tension emanating from him, and she wondered if he too
was besieged with doubts.

Did he wish that he was marrying Donata rather than a
woman he believed was as unscrupulous as his stepmother?
He had made no further reference to Donata, and although his
sister Jocasta was attending the wedding, there was no sign
of his beautiful cousin. But Tamsin could not forget the tri-
umphant gleam in Donata's eyes when she had emerged from
Bruno's bedroom in Florence, and was certain that she and
Bruno had been lovers.

The thought was agony, and she blinked hard to dispel her
tears as the registrar pronounced them man and wife and Bruno
turned towards her, brushing his mouth briefly over hers in a
kiss that held neither passion or warmth. It was a fitting beginning to a marriage that was based on convenience rather than
love, Tamsin thought dismally. Her heart ached, but pride came
to her rescue and she pinned a bright smile on her face and
turned to receive the congratulations of their guests.

It was many hours later before Bruno's plane landed in
Florence and he settled Tamsin in his car for the last leg of
their journey to the Villa Rosala. In the dim interior she looked
pale and incredibly fragile, her long eyelashes making dark
crescents on her cheeks.

His mouth tightened. He had feared that the journey to the

villa would be too much. They should have stayed in Florence tonight and travelled on to the house in the morning, but for some reason Tamsin had adamantly refused to stay at the Florence apartment, and had seemed so upset at the idea that he had reluctantly given in.

It seemed irrational to him, but he'd blamed her sudden dislike of the apartment on the pregnancy hormones that had turned her from the cool, level-headed woman he had first met into an emotionally fragile mass of insecurities. She had experienced no more bleeding, thank God, but no amount of reassurance from medical experts had calmed her fears of suffering a miscarriage.

Perhaps it was natural for pregnant women to worry endlessly, he brooded, frustrated by his inability to help her and her refusal to confide her concerns to him. Instead she spent a lot of time in her bedroom, clearly wanting to avoid him. Usually he had no patience for tears, but the sound of her weeping caused a peculiar pain in his gut. She hadn't smiled once since he had made the arrangements for their wedding, and he guessed her tears were because she hadn't wanted to marry him—but in that she had had no choice, he thought grimly. Because no child of his would be born illegitimate.

He swore beneath his breath and forced himself to concentrate on the narrow, twisting road that snaked though the dark Tuscan countryside. 'Not much further now,' he murmured when he felt Tamsin's eyes on him. 'You must be tired. It's been a long day.'

'Mmm.' But an unexpectedly lovely day, Tamsin mused, thinking back to the short but moving wedding ceremony, and the celebratory lunch afterwards at a nearby hotel.

All her family had been there—her sister Vicky looking heavily pregnant—and Jess had been her maid of honour, and spent most of her time bickering with Daniel, as usual. It was amazing how two intelligent people could be so blind, Tamsin thought sleepily. She liked the idea of having Jess for a sister-in-law; she just wished the two of them would stop fighting and recognise that they were attracted to each other.

'I loved the flowers,' she said to Bruno, recalling the profusion of pink and cream roses and lilies whose exquisite perfume had filled the register office. 'I thought Mum must have ordered them, but she was as surprised as me.'

'I'm glad you liked them, *cara*.' The amusement in Bruno's voice caused her heart to skip a beat.

'You mean…you? Why?' she faltered. 'I mean, thank you—they were beautiful… But you didn't have to. I didn't expect anything.'

'No,' Bruno said in a curiously, dry tone. 'I have come to realise that you have very few expectations.'

Any other woman would have demanded that the wedding take place at some grand location, followed by a lavish reception as befitted his billion-pound fortune. Tamsin had asked for nothing other than the attendance of her family and close friends, and he had even had to bully her into choosing a wedding ring from a top Hatton Garden jewellers. After considerable arguing she had eventually settled for a narrow plain gold band, and he was sure she had chosen it because it was one of the least expensive rings in the shop.

As if she could read his mind, she suddenly said, 'You don't have to wear your ring. I wasn't sure if you would want one or not. I mean…' she shifted restlessly in her seat, sounding as if she wished she had never started the conversation '…it's not as though ours is a normal marriage, and you might not want to advertise the fact that you have a wife.'

Tamsin had a stark image in her head of him chatting up gorgeous women at the nightclubs in Florence, his ringless finger advertising that he was a free agent, and a heavy weight settled in her chest. Bruno had a reputation as a playboy. He was hardly likely to curtail his socialising because he had acted honourably and married the woman who was expecting his child.

'I am quite happy for the world to know I am married,' he murmured coolly, 'and I will be honoured to wear my wedding ring.'

He swung the car through the gates of the Villa Rosala, his mind dwelling on Tamsin's assertion that their marriage was not a 'normal' one, and wondering why he wanted to smash his fist into the thick stone walls of the villa.

The house looked warm and inviting, with golden lamplight spilling from the downstairs windows. It had been his childhood home—a place of love and happiness before the bitter dispute that had divided him and his father. But now it was going to be a family home again—if he had not completely wrecked his marriage before it had even begun, he thought grimly.

He pulled up on the drive and cut the engine, but instead of getting out of the car he turned his head to Tamsin, unable to hold back the question that had been eating away at him ever since his conversation with James Grainger shortly before the wedding.

'Why didn't you tell me about James?'

Beside him, Tamsin stiffened. 'Tell you what about James?'

'That he has cancer. That the reason he went to London every week was to attend hospital and receive treatment. And that his chemotherapy left him feeling so weak that he relied on your help,' Bruno finished tensely.

'How do you know all this? Do Annabel and Davina know about James's illness?' Tamsin queried sharply.

'I assume so. He told me that Davina went with him on his recent visit to the specialist.'

'Thank goodness,' Tamsin murmured. 'I begged him to tell them before, but he was determined to deal with it without worrying them, and he didn't want anyone to know he had cancer.'

'Apart from you,' Bruno said quietly.

'Yes, but it's not what you think,' Tamsin replied quickly, her heart sinking at Bruno's grim expression. He already believed she had befriended James because he was a wealthy widower—what would he think of her now he knew James was suffering from a potentially life-threatening disease? 'James and I became friends when he hired me to design Davina and Hugo's flat,' she explained. 'I think he confided in me because he had no one else he could talk to. He was desperate to save his daughters from more worry when they were still grieving for their mother, but he could discuss his fears with me, confident that I would never betray his secret.'

Bruno's jaw tightened. 'Your loyalty is commendable, *bella*. You allowed me to think the worst of you, to accuse you of being a gold-digger like my step-mother, and you never attempted to defend yourself by explaining the real reason for your meetings with James in London.'

'I couldn't,' Tamsin said simply. 'I promised James.' She hesitated, and then muttered, 'Even if I had told you, I don't think you would have believed me. From the outset you were determined to think the worst of me. When you looked at me you saw your stepmother, and because you couldn't punish her for wrecking your relationship with your father, you punished me.'

'That's not true,' Bruno growled angrily. 'There were many pointers that proved you were like Miranda, and I don't deny I was determined to save James from making the same mistakes my father made. The old man who made you the beneficiary of his will—' Bruno broke off and raked his hand

through his hair. 'Your father told me today that you put most
of the money you inherited into a charity that organises care
for the elderly, to enable them to live in their own homes.'

Tamsin shrugged awkwardly. 'I spent some of it on me. I
paid for Jess and I to go on holiday—she stuck by me through
my darkest days after my marriage ended and I wanted to
thank her—and I bought some new clothes. My confidence
took a battering when Neil left me, and I suppose I was trying
to re-invent myself. I didn't marry him for his money, you
know. I married him because I loved him. But I have no idea
why he married me,' she said bitterly, 'because he was unfaithful from the day we returned from our honeymoon until the
day he walked out and moved in with his mistress.'

She opened the car door and stepped onto the drive, drawing
her coat around her to shield her from the rain that had been
falling since they had arrived in Italy. 'I'm glad James told you
the truth. He still faces an uncertain future, and he needs the
support of his friends. I swear I'm not like your stepmother
Bruno. I've never wanted anything from you.' Apart from your
love, she thought silently. But his face was a hard, arrogant
mask, and even though he now knew that she hadn't planned
to fleece a vulnerable widower, she could detect no softening
in his attitude towards her. Suddenly she felt desperately tired
and dejected, and her shoulders slumped. 'We're married now
and I suppose we'll just have to get on with it,' she muttered.

Bruno gave her a sharp stare as he rounded the car. 'As you
say, we'll just have to get on with it,' he drawled sardonically,
lifting her effortlessly into his arms and ignoring her
murmured protest that she weighed a ton as he carried her
through the front door. 'This is where you belong now
Tamsin. You and my son. It's true that the only reason we
married is for our baby's sake, but I swear I will do everything
in my power to make you and our child happy.'

Bruno's dark eyes burned into hers, and his vow seemed to echo around the hall of the villa, but his words enveloped Tamsin in a black cloak of despair. She was well aware that he had only married her because of the baby, but she didn't need to have him spell it out quite so brutally.

Would he have been so determined to marry her if she was expecting a girl? Of course he would, she acknowledged heavily. He had not even asked to know the sex of their child—but, having safely passed the fifteen-week landmark, she had begun to believe that she would carry this baby full-term, and had been eager to know as much as possible about the child she was carrying inside her.

Bruno was undoubtedly delighted that they were going to have a son. He had gone rather quiet and given her an odd look when she had shyly suggested that he might want to name the baby after his father, but little Stefano was the only reason she was here in the house she had designed and fallen in love with almost as much as she loved its master. And she would be happy, she told herself fiercely.

But as she stared into Bruno's beautiful sculpted face it was hard to see how—because there was always going to be something missing.

She swallowed the lump that had formed in her throat and gave a theatrical yawn. 'If you don't mind, I think I'll go straight to bed. I'm exhausted—what with travelling and everything,' she finished lamely, when Bruno's mouth thinned.

'You were the one who insisted on driving down to the villa. I would have been quite happy to stay at the apartment tonight, *bella*.'

Tamsin said nothing, but paled at the memory of how she had met his cousin emerging from the master bedroom of his bachelor pad. She stroked her hand over the firm swell of her stomach, as if to reassure herself of the presence of her baby, and Bruno's eyes followed her movements. The atmosphere in the hall changed imperceptibly, and as his eyes became slumberous beneath his heavy lids, she felt a quiver low in her pelvis.

It felt strangely surreal to be back at the villa. The last time she had been here they had spent practically every waking hour making wild, tempestuous love. Now she was over four months pregnant, and they were married, but it was not a conventional marriage and she didn't know if Bruno expected to consummate their unconventional relationship.

His expression was unreadable as his eyes moved from her rounded belly to her breasts, which were now full and heavy. She looked very different from when she had last shared his bed, she thought on a wave of fear. What if he took her to bed and was revolted by her pregnant body? Or compared her curvaceous breasts and hips with Donatella's model-thin figure? The thought was unbearable, and when he moved towards her she took a jerky step backwards.

'I really am tired,' she said in a thin, sharp voice. 'I thought perhaps I could have the room I slept in when I first came to work here?' Bruno's silent, narrow-eyed scrutiny unnerved her, and when he lifted a hand to her she visibly flinched, and admitted in a panic-filled tone, 'I don't know what you expect from me. I know at my last antenatal appointment, the doctor said that my pregnancy is progressing fine,' she continued shakily, 'and that there is no reason for us not to…well, you know…' She tailed to a halt, her face burning as she recalled the doctor's blunt statement that it was perfectly safe for them to have sex. Bruno had been sitting next to her, and when they'd left the surgery she had wanted to die of embarrassment, but to her relief he had not mentioned the subject, or attempted to make love to her.

It wasn't that she didn't want him to. Now that her sickness had stopped she was feeling incredibly fit and energetic—and shockingly turned on. He had told her that the amazing sex they enjoyed was as good a basis as any for marriage, and if his body was the only thing he would share with her, she would take it.

Her nights were tormented by fantasies of Bruno exploring every sensitive dip and curve of her body, before moving over her and entering her with deep, powerful thrusts. She longed for him to take her in his arms and lead her along that wickedly pleasurable path to sexual ecstasy, and sometimes she caught him looking at her in a way that made her think he wanted her too. But then she would remember Donata's exotic beauty and stunning body, and her doubts would return.

Bruno dropped his hand to his side and snatched up Tamsin's travel bag, determined to control the shaft of blinding anger that surged through him. 'I don't expect anything from you,' he informed her in a clipped tone. 'Certainly nothing that you are not willing to give, *bella*. But I'm afraid you'll have to share my bed tonight. Your clothes and belongings arrived here a couple of days ago, and Battista has put them all in the master bedroom. I fear she has a romantic streak, and believes that as we are now man and wife we will be sleeping in the same room. I'll leave you to disabuse her of the notion,' he said tightly as he shepherded her up the stairs. 'In the meantime, fortunately my bed is so big that if you keep to your side of the mattress you can pretend that I am not even there.'

The open sarcasm in his voice scraped Tamsin's already raw nerves, and when they reached the landing she spun away from him. 'I would still prefer to sleep in my own room. I tend to wriggle around a lot during the night, and I might disturb you,' she added, trying to prove to him how sensible it would be for them to have separate rooms.

'I think that's entirely likely, *cara*,' Bruno drawled in that same hatefully sardonic tone. 'But that is my problem. None of the guest beds are made up,' he told her firmly, gripping her arm and literally frogmarching her into the master bedroom.

His mouth tightened at the flare of panic in her eyes, and he dropped her travel bag onto the bed and strode back over to the door.

'Stop looking at me as though you're terrified I might murder you while you sleep,' he grated harshly. 'I have never taken a woman by force in my life, and I certainly don't intend to start with my pregnant wife. I have to make a couple of phone calls,' he continued in the same icy tone. 'I suggest you hurry up and get into bed. And for both our sakes let's hope you are asleep when I come back.'

Brilliant. They had only been married for a few hours, and already they weren't speaking, Tamsin brooded miserably as she trailed into the *en suite* bathroom. She was tempted to defy him and sleep in another room, but the thought of finding sheets and bedding and making up a bed was too much. It had been a long and emotionally draining day, and her body ached with exhaustion. She unzipped her travel bag, and frowned when she lifted out a flat package wrapped in tissue paper.

'Your wedding present is in your overnight bag,' Jess had whispered in her ear, when she and Bruno had taken leave of their guests after the celebratory wedding lunch.

Tamsin had assumed the gift was perfume or, knowing Jess's quirky sense of humour, a musical toothbrush, and tears filled her eyes when she unfolded a gossamer-fine ivory silk nightgown. Further searching in her bag revealed that Jess had removed the oversized tee shirt she had packed and, cursing and loving her friend in equal measures, she slipped the nightgown over her head.

At four and a half months pregnant, she had not expected to look sexy, but the diaphanous material skimmed her bump, while the lacy bodice plunged low to reveal the new fullness of her breasts. Jess had clearly bought it with seduction in mind, but all that was in Tamsin's mind was racing into bed and ensuring she was hidden beneath the covers before Bruno returned.

She was too late. When she walked back into the bedroom and saw him sprawled indolently on the vast bed, her heart jerked painfully in her chest. He had removed his tie and unfastened his shirt buttons to the waist, revealing his muscular olive-skinned chest, covered with a mass of wiry, black hairs that arrowed down beneath the waistband of his trousers. Who had he needed to speak to on his wedding night? Tamsin wondered, feeling the familiar sick jealousy burn like acid in her stomach. Had he phoned Donata? Or did he have another mistress in Florence? He was so gorgeous it was impossible to believe he had been celibate in the weeks between her departure from Tuscany and meeting him at his London office to tell him she was pregnant.

Tamsin hovered uncertainly in the doorway, and Bruno's eyes narrowed as he stared at her gorgeous, lush curves and felt his body's instant, throbbing response. He longed to tug her down onto the bed and remove the tantalising wisp of transparent silk that brushed against her thighs and cupped her breasts, displaying them like plump, ripe peaches. He wanted to discover every inch of her voluptuous body and bury his face against her satin soft, delicately scented flesh—but he knew that he had no right to touch her, and the guilt that had been steadily intensifying inside him since his conversation with James Grainger rose up and threatened to choke him.

'Come and get into bed,' he said quietly, drawing back the covers. 'You look exhausted, *cara,* and that's not good for the baby.'

And of course the baby was all he was interested in—which was just as it should be, Tamsin told herself as she slid into bed and tugged the sheet up to her chin. Clearly the sexy nightdress had failed to disguise the fact that she looked fat and tired. She really didn't know why she cared, or why tears were burning her eyes. She squeezed them shut, praying that Bruno would think she was already asleep when he emerged from the bathroom.

Several minutes later the mattress dipped, and she heard the dry amusement in his voice as he leaned over her and dropped a brief, tantalising kiss on her lips. 'Asleep so soon? You *were* tired. Sweet dreams, *bella mia*.'

With about an acre of mattress between them, she had no idea what, if anything, he was wearing in bed, but the idea that he could be lying naked next to her caused liquid heat to flood through her veins, and it seemed impossible that sleep would ever relieve her of the restless desire that made her muscles ache. Her mind re-ran their wedding ceremony at the register office until her thoughts became fuzzy and sleep claimed her.

Suddenly she wasn't in the register office, but a church. Bruno was striding down the aisle, away from the altar, and she was running after him, sobbing his name as she begged him not to leave her. But as she reached him he swung round, and it wasn't Bruno—it was…

'Neil!'

'*Madre de Dio*, Tamsin. Wake up. You can't keep getting upset like this—it can't be good for the baby.'

Slowly Tamsin opened her eyes and stared up at Bruno's grim face. Her cheeks were wet, and her throat felt as though she had swallowed glass, but her mind was clouded and she didn't know why she had been crying. 'I was dreaming,' she whispered, frowning as she tried to recall what about. It must have been the old recurring dream about losing her baby, she decided, scrubbing her eyes with the back of her hand. 'I'm sorry I disturbed you.' She had never seen Bruno look so furious, and she bit her lip. 'I told you I should have slept in another room.'

To her dismay, he did not argue. 'I'll have Battista prepare a room tomorrow,' he snapped. 'Go back to sleep now.'

Bruno rolled onto his side and switched off the bedside lamp, so that the room was plunged into a darkness that was as black and heavy as his mood. He felt a bitter, burning sensation in his gullet, as if he had drunk poison. Why the hell did it matter that she still dreamed of her ex-husband? he asked himself angrily. He had heard the pain in her voice earlier, when she'd told him how she had loved Neil Harper, and it was clear that his infidelity had broken her heart. Did she still have feelings for her ex, despite the despicable way he had treated her? Was that the reason her eyes had shimmered with tears when he had kissed her at the end of their wedding ceremony? She'd been wishing that it was Neil she had just promised to spend the rest of her life with rather than him?

But she had married *him*, Bruno thought savagely. She was expecting his child, and the health and well-being of his unborn son was the only thing he cared about. With that settled, he rolled onto his back and stared up at the ceiling, waiting for sleep. But it didn't come, and by dawn his eyes felt gritty and a lead weight seemed to have settled in his chest.

CHAPTER TWELVE

WHEN Tamsin opened her eyes the next morning she found she was alone, and the only sign that Bruno had slept beside her all night was a faint indentation on his pillow. She wondered if he was still annoyed with her for waking him in the night. She couldn't even remember the dream that had left her sobbing. It had certainly been a traumatic wedding night—but for all the wrong reasons, she acknowledged dismally, recalling his tight-lipped expression when he had shaken her awake.

She could hear rain hammering against the window, and when she pulled back the curtains the Tuscan countryside was hidden behind a veil of grey mist. The river that usually gurgled gently at the side of the house was fuller than she had ever seen it, and white frothy waves danced across the surface as it hurtled down into the valley.

Bruno was in the kitchen when she went downstairs. He looked remote and forbidding, in black jeans and a matching jumper, but heart-stoppingly sexy, with his hair falling onto his brow and faint dark stubble shading his jaw. Tamsin was immediately conscious that her loose-fitting trousers and tunic top were hardly a turn-on, and she quickly subsided into a chair opposite him at the table, so that he couldn't see her swollen stomach.

'You're going to be twice the size you are now,' her mother had laughingly informed her when they had been shopping for her wedding outfit.

Tamsin felt quite happy about the visible sign that her little son was growing bigger, but from Bruno's expression she was sure he found her lack of waistline unattractive, and she wished he would stop looking at her.

'You'd better decide which room you want,' he said tersely, while he poured her a glass of fruit juice and buttered one of the still-warm rolls that the housekeeper must have baked that morning. 'I'll leave you to explain to Battista why you are moving into your own room, and she can carry your things. You are not to get over-tired,' he warned her as he handed her the roll and passed her the cherry jam that he knew was her favourite. 'Anyway, there's no rush. I'm going back to Florence. I have an early meeting tomorrow morning,' he continued at her obvious surprise, 'and I have some paperwork to catch on first. After that I'm flying to Paris, and then Amsterdam, and I won't be back until the end of the week. So you'll be quite safe to sleep in my bed for the next few nights.'

She flushed at the mockery in his tone and put down the roll after one bite, as the image of him rushing back to meet Donata at his apartment destroyed her appetite. 'I'll move my things into another room as soon as you've gone,' she said stonily. 'I want my own space.'

'As you wish.' Bruno scraped back his chair and stood up. 'I'll go now, and then you'll have all the space you could possibly wish for.' He thrust his arms into his leather jacket and stood towering over her, so impossibly beautiful that Tamsin longed to throw herself into his arms and beg him to stay with her. Their marriage had got off to a truly terrible start, and she had no idea how to retrieve the situation.

'It's lucky we didn't arrange a honeymoon if you're so busy

at work,' she muttered, knowing she sounded like a petulant teenager, but unable to stop herself.

Bruno turned in the doorway and glared at her. 'A honeymoon is the usual way to start normal married life, I agree. But, as you pointed out, *bella,* our marriage is far from normal. Our wedding night was evidence of that.'

'You mean because we didn't have sex?' Tamsin flung at him, stung by his implied accusation that she hadn't delivered the goods on their wedding night.

'I mean because you spent the night dreaming about your ex-husband,' Bruno replied icily, before he strode out and slammed the front door so hard that the villa trembled on its foundations.

What on earth did he mean? Tamsin moved to the window and watched listlessly as he hurtled down the drive so fast that the car's tyres squealed on the wet gravel. Neil was the last person she would ever dream about—although he had featured in a few of her nightmares. She could almost believe that Bruno had sounded jealous, but now she really was entering the realms of fantasy, she acknowledged as she headed back upstairs. She didn't know if he really had an early business meeting tomorrow, or whether he was racing off to see his mistress, and although she told herself she didn't care, she could not hold back her tears as she buried her face on his pillow and wept for everything that their marriage could have been if only he had loved her.

After a couple of hours she pulled herself together and wandered aimlessly around the empty house, before picking out a room along the corridor from the master bedroom that had an *en suite* bathroom and an additional dressing room that she decided would make an ideal nursery for Stefano. She already had a few ideas about a soft blue colour scheme and a hand-painted border, but after another fruitless hour she gave up trying to sketch her plans.

Back in the kitchen, Battista looked unusually harassed, and Tamsin immediately decided to postpone asking the housekeeper to help her move her belongings out of Bruno's room until another day.

'This rain is bad,' Battista said worriedly, wringing her hands when Tamsin asked what was wrong. 'Down in the valley the river is close to spilling out,' she explained in her broken English. 'If it does it will flood the village, and my daughter's house is right in its path.' The older woman wiped her eyes on her apron. 'I'm scared for Carissa and the *bambini*. Carlo is only a few months old, and the little girls will be so frightened. Guido would go for them, but he has hurt his back and has to lie still.' More tears slid down her wrinkled face, and Tamsin instinctively hugged her.

'I'll go and get your daughter and her family and bring them back here. The Villa Rosala is on a hill, and I imagine we're safe from flooding here,' she added as she stared out at the torrential rain. She prayed that Bruno had reached Florence safely. Maybe she would ring him later. And if Donata answered, well—her heart lurched at the thought—at least she would know why Bruno had driven off in such a hurry.

She pushed the familiar pang of jealousy to one side and smiled reassuringly at Battista, who was shaking her head.

'You can't go. Signor Di Cesare would never allow it.'

'Well, he isn't here, so he won't know, will he? Please don't worry, Battista. I'll take Guido's car, and I'll be back with Carissa and the children in no time.'

Bruno stared blankly at his computer screen and realised that he had read the same paragraph of legal jargon three times. He seemed incapable of concentrating on the finer details of the exciting new business deal that he had spent months setting up and which he was now close to completing. Even worse, he couldn't care less if the House of Di Cesare opened a new flagship store on the Avenue des Champs-Elysées in the heart of Paris.

He didn't care about anything, he acknowledged heavily. At least he didn't care about any of the things that had previously been important to him—predominantly work, the company, and his determination to atone for his father's failures in the last years of his life and make the House of Di Cesare a world market leader. Under his leadership the company was already enjoying phenomenal success, but he felt weary and defeated—as if he had fallen into a deep well of despair and could not summon the energy to climb out.

In another few months his son would be born, he reminded himself. He would be a father to little Stefano, and he was determined to be a good father—like his father had been to him. But, unlike his father, he would never allow anyone to come between him and his son.

His child would be the most important thing in his life. That was the reason he had married Tamsin—the only reason, he told himself fiercely. But as he got to his feet and stared out over the dark, rain-lashed city he knew he was lying to himself.

The knowledge that he had misjudged her was eating away at him. He had been wrong about her. He had leapt to conclusions based on his past rather than logical thought, and he had treated her so badly that it was little wonder she had spent the weeks running up to their wedding weeping and trying to avoid him.

Was there any possibility of salvaging their marriage? When he had driven her down to the villa he had been cautiously optimistic that he would be able to make his peace with her, apologise for the way he had treated her and re-establish the tenuous friendship that had developed between them while they had been lovers. But that was before he'd discovered that she still dreamed about her ex-husband.

Why should he care if Tamsin was still in love with Neil Harper? he brooded as he paced the floor of his study and raked his hand through his hair until it stood on end. At least it negated any possibility that she might fall in love with *him*.

The knock on his study door dragged him from his bitter thoughts, and he forced a smile for his butler. 'Salvatore, how are you? I am sorry to hear about your mother. Did all your family return to Sicily for the funeral?'

'*Si*—it went well. My mother would have been pleased at the turn-out,' Salvatore replied gravely. '*Signor*, I have not seen you since your trip to the US—I went back to Sicily before you returned—but…' The butler hesitated, and then said, 'There is something I must tell you.'

Two hours later Bruno screeched to a halt in front of the Villa Rosala and leapt out of the car. Rain lashed his face as he ran towards the house, and above the noise of the wind he could hear the angry sounds of the river as it crashed down the hillside. Thank God his ancestors had built the villa here at the top of the valley, away from danger if the river burst its banks. Lights from the windows made the villa glow like a beacon of warmth in the gathering dusk, and some of his tension left him as he thought of Tamsin curled up safe and warm in front of the fire in the sitting room.

He would have been here sooner if he had not wasted precious minutes on the phone, furiously warning his cousin Donata that if she ever lied to, or even spoke to his wife again he would cut off the monthly allowance that she received from the Di Cesare fortune. He had no idea why Donata had made up her fantastic tale that they were engaged. He'd never given any indication that he wanted a relationship with her, let alone marry her, but she had always been a spoilt bitch. He did not care if she was the only other great-grandchild of Antonio Di Cesare—he would be quite happy if he never set eyes on her again.

But Tamsin did not know that Donata's claim had been pure fantasy. He had been mildly irritated when Donata had turned up at his apartment the night before he had flown to the US, with some story about a broken love-affair, and had pleaded with him to allow her to stay. He had left at dawn the following day to catch his flight. But according to his butler Donata had gone to his room in the early hours, dressed—as Salvatore had so delicately put it—like a woman of the streets, and been furious when she'd discovered that he had already gone. When Tamsin arrived at the apartment a short while later, Salvatore had said, Donata had clearly implied that she had spent the night with Bruno, and Tamsin had looked—in Salvatore's words—heartbroken.

Why had Tamsin gone to the apartment? Bruno wondered curiously. Had she intended to tell him to his face that she was returning to England and her career? Or had there been another reason for her visit? Suddenly it seemed imperative that he know the truth, and he strode into the villa, unable to control his urgent need to see her.

He frowned when his housekeeper, Battista, hurried into the hall. She had clearly been crying, and at his terse, 'Where is Signora Di Cesare?' more tears poured down her cheeks. It took endless moments and all of his patience before he finally learned that Tamsin had driven down to the village in search of Battista's daughter, and as he recalled the wild night, and the angry, churning river, an icy feeling of dread filled him.

'I don't know what has happened.' Battista stumbled after him as he turned back towards the front door. 'The telephone is not working, and the *signora*, she left hours ago.'

Bruno did not hear his housekeeper's sobs. He was already behind the wheel of his car and driving as fast as the dire conditions would allow along the steep, narrow road leading down to the village. The gleam from the headlights cut through the dark, and as he turned a corner and saw Guido's familiar little car, upended and partially submerged in the river, his blood turned cold.

'*Madre de Dio,* Tamsin, where are you?' He shouted her name over and over, his stomach churning as terror unlike anything he had ever felt in his life gripped him. She did not answer and, slipping and sliding on the mud, he scoured the banks with his torch until the ever-rising waters of the swollen river forced him back to his car, before it too was swept away.

Why had she come out in the storm when she must have realised that the river was dangerously close to bursting its banks? It was sheer madness. But as soon as she had heard that Battista's grandchildren were at risk she would have been determined to help, Bruno acknowledged grimly. Far from being the callous, unscrupulous woman he had believed, she possessed—as James Grainger had stated—the most generous heart of anyone he had ever met. It was a pity he had not realised it sooner, he thought savagely, because there was no sign of her by the river, and sick fear gagged his throat as he faced the knowledge that he might be too late.

Somehow he managed to drive on into the village, heading for the town hall where lights and voices indicated that many of the villagers had taken refuge there.

'Have you seen my wife? Signora Di Cesare—she is English, blonde hair…' He pushed his way through the throng of frightened people into the hall, his heart pounding. She *had* to be here. They *had not* drowned in the river—Tamsin and his unborn son. His life would not be worth living without them—without her.

He acknowledged the blinding truth on a wave of sheer, agonised fear as he scanned the packed room. *'Tamsin! Where the hell are you?'*

'Bruno—I'm here.'

The small, hesitant voice sounded from behind him, and he spun round and stared at her—covered from head to toe in mud, so it was not surprising he hadn't recognised her.

She was sitting with Battista's daughter and her children, smiling at Carissa's baby. *Smiling,* he noted savagely, as he swallowed the constriction in his throat and felt an unfamiliar burning sensation behind his eyelids. She was smiling while he had been going out of his mind.

'Tesoro…' He reached for her blindly. His vision seemed to be blurred, and as he drew her small, muddy form into his arms and held her close to his heart, the dam that had held back his emotions for so long broke, and he buried his face in her hair, his chest heaving.

'Bruno…darling—don't.' Tamsin's voice cracked. 'Stefano is fine; he's been kicking like mad. Here.' She guided his hand to her stomach. 'Can you feel him? I'm sorry,' she whispered, visibly shocked by the betraying wetness on his face. 'I know you must have been terrified to think you had lost him.'

'I thought I had lost both of you,' Bruno admitted harshly.

Relief surged through him, robbing him of his voice, and he did not add that if she had been swept away in the river he would thrown himself in after her. He claimed her lips in a gentle, evocative kiss that tasted of mud and tears, although he did not know if they were hers or his. Tamsin was staring up at him as if he had lost his mind. And perhaps he had, he thought as he lifted her into his arms and began to make his way out of the hall. What other explanation could there be for the madness that filled him with a wild euphoria? He did not believe in love, but everything that was dear to him was here in his arms, and he would never, ever let her go.

Afterwards Tamsin could not remember much about the journey back to the Villa Rosala, but the sight of Guido's car in the river brought back those terrible moments when she had feared for her life and that of her baby.

'It's over now, *cara*, and you are safe—thank God,' Bruno grated harshly, when he heard her murmur of distress, and then they were home, and he was carrying her up the stairs while Battista clung to her daughter and grandchildren, who had travelled up to the villa with them in the back of Bruno's car.

He said nothing as he stripped her out of her sodden, muddy clothes before removing his own, but his eyes flared with answering hunger when he caught her unguarded look of desire. 'Later, *cara mia*,' he promised softly as he joined her in the shower. 'But first we need to get you clean. You don't smell too good, *bella*,' he teased, and watched her eyes darken as he smoothed the soap over her breasts and the firm swell of her stomach.

'Don't—I look fat,' Tamsin whispered in an agony of embarrassment, but Bruno drew her hands down from where she had tried to hide her shape from him and stared at her, dull colour streaking along his cheekbones as the hard length of his arousal nudged her thighs.

'You are pregnant with my son,' he said rawly, 'and you have never looked more beautiful than you do now.'

'Bruno—kiss me, please.' Tonight she had thought that her life was over, but by some miracle she had managed to squeeze out of the window before the car was sucked beneath the water, and swim against the ferocious current to the shore. She had been given a second chance at life, and pride had no place in it

When he reached for her she opened her arms and slid them around his waist, while he moved his mouth on hers in a shattering kiss of pure possession. It was bliss when she had been starved of him for so long, and she melted against him, uncaring that her fevered response to him revealed the secrets of her heart. She opened her mouth, eagerly welcoming the bold thrust of his tongue as he deepened the kiss to another level, but then, despite the fact that they were both shaking with need, he stepped out of the shower, enfolded her in a towel and carried her into the bedroom.

He placed her on the bed as carefully as if she was made of delicate porcelain, but to Tamsin's disappointment, instead of joining her, he donned his robe and moved towards the door.

'I'll leave you to get dry, *cara,* while I make you some tea. You must be in shock after tonight,' he explained, a curious note in his voice as he added, 'I need to take care of you.'

She didn't want him to take care of her. She wanted him to make wild, passionate love to her, Tamsin thought dismally. But of course what Bruno really meant was that he wanted to take care of his baby—although Stefano seemed none the worse for the trauma she had put him through, and from his energetic kicking definitely had a future career with the Italian football team.

She dried her hair, so that it fell in a curtain of gold silk around her shoulders, and slipped the nightgown that Jess had bought her over her head before she climbed into bed. She wondered if Bruno expected her to have moved into her own room—as she had told him she would during their last bitter exchange before he had driven back to Florence. If so, he was going to be disappointed, because she was his wife and she belonged in his bed—and even the spectre of his beautiful cousin would not detract her from her determination to fight for him.

Her eyes flew to his face when he returned a few minutes

later, bearing a tea tray, and her heartbeat quickened when he stretched out on the bed next to her. Her senses flared at his closeness, and she took a gulp of the hot, sweet tea and tried not to imagine his naked body hidden beneath his robe.

Now that she was safe she kept re-running everything that had happened down in the village, but for some reason her mind locked on the expression she had seen on his face when he had first spotted her in the village town hall. His patent relief had been mixed with another, indefinable emotion that had made her hope… But then she had reminded herself that his concern was for their child. Now that look was back in his eyes, and she was shaking so much that she had to put down her tea before she spilt it.

'There is something I have to know Tamsin,' he said quietly as he lifted her hand and stroked his thumb-pad over the pulse jerking frantically in her wrist. 'Why did you go to the apartment on the morning that I flew to the States?'

'How did you—?' She broke off and bit her lip. 'Salvatore told you, I suppose?'

Bruno nodded. 'He told me that you met my cousin.' When she made no reply he tipped her chin and stared into her eyes, an emotion she did not recognise blazing in his midnight-dark gaze. 'Donata lied to you, *cara*. I did not sleep with her that night, or any other night. There has never been anything between us.'

'But she said you intended to marry her to strengthen the Di Cesare bloodline,' Tamsin faltered. 'She also said that you had a weakness for blondes, and I was just another in a long line of women who had graced your bed and meant nothing to you. But of course I already knew that,' she added thickly.

Bruno made a harsh sound low in his throat and sprang up from the bed, moving jerkily instead of with his usual lithe grace. He paced the room restlessly for several moments, before he swung back to face her, his expression so tortured that Tamsin caught her breath.

'You were right when you said I was determined to think the worst of you,' he said abruptly. 'I had suspicions about the reason for your friendship with James Grainger. But if I had been behaving logically I would have had you properly investigated, spoken to people who knew you—maybe even spoken to James about my concerns,' he added with a humourless smile. 'But I took one look at you at Davina's wedding and I knew you were trouble. Not for James,' he continued relentlessly when she opened her mouth to protest, 'but for me.'

He walked back over to the bed and stood staring down at her, his eyes narrowed on her face.

'Did you go to Florence because you hoped to see me?' he demanded, his eyes burning into hers as if he was determined to read her mind.

A few moments ago she had vowed to forgo her pride, but now her courage seemed to be deserting her. She hesitated, and then lifted her chin. 'Yes. I wanted…I was going to tell you that I had decided to stay on at the villa with you. I had no expectations that we had any sort of future together—not when you mistrusted me as you did,' she said huskily. 'But I wanted to be with you and nothing else seemed to matter.'

'But instead you met Donata, and believed her lies,' Bruno said flatly.

'She was very convincing.' Tamsin swallowed hard. 'And it seemed entirely likely that you had another mistress. Neil was repeatedly unfaithful when I was married to him. And you and I—well, you had never made any promises,' she added quietly. 'Neil destroyed my self-respect with his lies, and I…I thought you were the same as him.'

'I am nothing like your ex-husband,' Bruno grated impatiently. 'And after what you've told me about him, I can't believe you're still in love with him.'

Tamsin stared at him in astonishment. 'I don't love Neil.'

'Then why do you still dream of him? Why did you call his name in the middle of the night and weep when it was me who tried to comfort you, not him? *Dio,* you cried every day before our wedding because you wished you were still with him, rather than about to marry me.' He threw her a furious look. 'I have even wondered if you wish you were carrying his child rather than mine.'

He was breathing hard, and abruptly swung away from her, but not before Tamsin glimpsed the flash of raw pain in his eyes. She shook her head slowly, trying to make sense of his words.

'You're wrong, Bruno, I don't dream about Neil. I remember now that when I said his name last night I had been dreaming that you were leaving me. I was crying, but when I reached you, it was Neil, and I realised that I had never loved him at all. As for carrying his child—I did once—for fifteen weeks,' she whispered. 'I was devastated when I discovered that Neil was having an affair. I already knew that he wouldn't be pleased about the baby, and I'd been worried about telling him. We'd agreed to wait a couple of years before thinking about a family and my pregnancy was an accident. But I still hoped…'

Her voice faltered. 'I hoped that he would end his affair and stay with me and the baby. Instead he was furious—told me he didn't want our child, that fatherhood didn't fit in with his career plans, and he was going to file for a divorce.' She closed her eyes briefly. 'He then suggested that I should abort our child. I moved out that day—I couldn't bear to remain in the house we had shared. I rented a flat, and a few weeks later I suffered a miscarriage.' Her fatalistic shrug masked the pain that had never left her. 'So in a way Neil got his wish—there was no baby. I know you must have found my constant crying irritating,' she murmured, flushing beneath his hard stare. 'But being pregnant again brought back all the feelings I'd had when I lost my first baby, and I was so scared I would lose this little one too. I certainly wasn't crying over Neil,' she added sharply, and then queried in a puzzled voice, 'But even if I did dream of him, why would you care?'

For a moment it seemed that Bruno would not answer. He had moved over to the window, and stood staring out at the wild night, his shoulders rigid with tension. But suddenly he jerked his head round, his dark eyes blazing and the same tortured expression he had worn earlier making deep grooves on either side of his mouth.

'Because I love you, *tesoro*.' The words were deep and low, and shaking with such emotion that Tamsin felt as though her heart had stopped. 'Although, God forgive me, I did not want to,' he admitted rawly. 'I experienced first-hand the destructive power of love. I watched my father's obsession with Miranda destroy him, and I was determined that no woman would ever have such a hold over me.' He walked back over to the bed, his eyes never leaving hers, and with every step he took Tamsin's heart beat a little faster. 'And then I met you.'

'And immediately decided I was a gold-digger, like your stepmother,' Tamsin said on a shaken voice.

'I think I knew almost from the beginning that you were nothing like Miranda,' he said sombrely. 'But I had to believe it. It was like a talisman—if I believed you were like Miranda, I couldn't love you. I refused to be a weak fool like my father, and I fought my feelings for you—convinced myself that what we shared was just blindingly good sex.' His mouth curved into a rueful smile, and for the first time Tamsin felt a faint, tremulous hope that this was real and not some cruel practical joke. 'I should have known that it was only that good because when I made love to you it was with my heart as well as my body,' Bruno added fiercely.

Oh, God! He seemed to be waiting for her to say something, but the words were trapped inside her, and she tore her eyes from him and nervously pleated the bedspread between her fingers.

With a muttered imprecation he whipped the covers back and sat down next to her. The month that we lived here together as lovers—you were happy,' he said gruffly. 'I can make you happy again, Tamsin.' He reached out and traced his finger down her cheek before cupping her jaw in his palm. 'When you left me I told myself I was glad, and I was determined to forget you. But you dominated my thoughts and haunted my dreams, and when you came to me in London and announced that you were carrying my child, it gave me the excuse I needed to force you back into my life—this time for good.'

'Bruno…' She still could not comprehend that he loved her. 'You married me because you wanted your son.'

'No, I married you because I wanted you—*want* you—will always want you,' he said, in the same harsh tone that she suddenly realised masked the fierce storm-force of emotions he was battling to control. He brought his other hand up to smooth her hair back from her face and she saw that his fingers were shaking. 'Give me one more chance,' he said, and now his voice was urgent, desperate, and it tore at her heart. 'I know you've been hurt in the past, and that you never deserved my appalling treatment of you. But I love you more than life, *tesoro*, and if you let me, I will teach you to love me.'

Even when he was trying to be humble he sounded arrogantly sure of himself, and of his ability to bend her to his will, but the faint wariness in his eyes and the rigid set of his jaw spoke of a vulnerability that broke through the last of Tamsin's defences.

'Darling Bruno…' She traced the shape of his mouth as she

had longed to do all that time ago, when they had met at Davina Grainger's wedding. It seemed incredible that this proud, uncompromising, awesome man was actually begging for the chance to persuade her to love him, but the raw emotion in his eyes was real, and she knew with a certainty that shook her that he would love her for ever.

'I don't need you to teach me to love you. I fell in love with you when I fell into your arms at Davina's wedding. And although there have been many times when I've hated you,' she said ruefully, 'I never stopped loving you and I never will. You are my life,' she told him fiercely, her voice suddenly strong as she sought to convince him that he was her reason for living. 'Love me, Bruno…'

She cradled his face in her hands and kissed him with all the pent-up love and passion that burned inside her, and he needed no second bidding as he ran his hands feverishly over her body.

'*Cara mia,* I don't deserve your love,' he said thickly. 'But I will cherish you and our son for the rest of my life. *Ti amo,* Tamsin. You don't know how many nights I have lain awake dreaming of this,' he growled in a low tone that throbbed with desire as he drew the straps of her nightgown down her arms so that her breasts spilled into his palms. 'I could *die* with wanting you.'

His tongue laved her sensitive swollen nipples, first one and then the other, until she arched beneath him and sobbed his name. When he stripped her completely some of her doubts returned, but he dealt with them by pressing hungry kisses over the firm mound of her stomach, telling her over and over how much he loved the fact that she was full and ripe with his child.

And then he moved lower, and Tamsin lost all sense of time and place as he gently pushed her thighs apart and stroked his tongue across her acutely sensitive clitoris, before probing deeper into the moist warmth of her vagina. When he moved over her and entered her with one firm, yet exquisitely tender thrust, he groaned her name and cupped her bottom as he set a rhythm that sent them spinning higher and higher towards heaven on earth.

Their loving was achingly familiar and yet wonderfully new as they finally spoke the words of love that had been locked away for so long. But then there was no time for words, just soft cries and deeper groans as Bruno's control shattered and he drove into her hard and fast, and Tamsin clung to him as wave after wave of incredible pleasure swept through her.

'Don't cry, *tesoro*,' he pleaded, when the last shudders of spent passion finally left him. He rolled onto his back, taking her with him so that she rested her head on his chest, and he felt her tears anoint his skin. 'Tonight I faced the utter desolation of thinking I had lost you for ever, but fate has given me a second chance and I will never let you go.' He brushed his lips over hers in a gentle benediction and said quietly, 'You have my heart, *cara*.'

Tamsin gave him a dazzling smile and wondered how it was possible to feel such happiness. 'And you have mine, my darling—for ever.'

EPILOGUE

STEFANO GIANCOMO DI CESARE entered the world on a beautiful spring day, after a short, uncomplicated labour, and promptly demonstrated that he had inherited his father's stubborn determination to have his own way, as well as a healthy set of lungs. Tamsin fell in love with him as instantly and as irrevocably as she had fallen in love with her husband, and was overjoyed when she and Bruno took their son home to the Villa Rosala.

'How do you like the idea of spending six weeks in the Bahamas?' Bruno queried, when Stefano had been settled in his crib and he was able to have Tamsin to himself for a couple of hours. 'I thought we could combine a honeymoon with our first family holiday—seeing that neither of us wants to be away from our son for more than five minutes,' he added with a wry smile.

He was happy to admit that he was as besotted with his baby son as he was with Tamsin, and he felt the familiar tug on his heart when she stretched up and pressed her mouth on his.

'It sounds wonderful. But I don't mind where we go as long as we're together,' she said seriously. She took one last peep into the crib and followed Bruno over to the bed. 'Stefano is so gorgeous, isn't he? In a year or so I'd really like to give him a little brother or sister. What do you think?'

Bruno was busy unbuttoning her blouse, and he gave her a wolfish smile as he tugged it from her shoulders before he unfastened her bra. 'Stefano is perfect. But I think we should put in plenty of practice in making babies, *cara*—starting right now.'

And as he drew her into the loving circle of his arms, Tamsin had to agree.

* * * * *

THOROUGHBRED LEGACY
*The stakes are high when it comes to love,
horse racing, family secrets
and broken promises.*

*A new exciting Harlequin continuity series coming soon!
Led by* New York Times *bestselling author
Elizabeth Bevarly
FLIRTING WITH TROUBLE*

Here's a preview

THE DOOR CLOSED behind them, throwing them into darkness and leaving them utterly alone. And the next thing Daniel knew, he heard himself saying, "Marnie, I'm sorry about the way things turned out in Del Mar."

She said nothing at first, only strode across the room and stared out the window beside him. Although he couldn't see her well in the darkness—he still hadn't switched on a light…but then, neither had she—he imagined her expression was a little preoccupied, a little anxious, a little confused.

Finally, very softly, she said, "Are you?"

He nodded, then, worried she wouldn't be able to see the gesture, added, "Yeah. I am. I should have said goodbye to you."

"Yes, you should have."

Actually, he thought, there were a lot of things he should have done in Del Mar. He'd had *a lot* riding on the Pacific Classic, and even more on his entry, Little Joe, but after meeting Marnie, the Pacific Classic had been the last thing on Daniel's mind. His loss at Del Mar had pretty much ended his career before it had even begun, and he'd had to start all over again, rebuilding from nothing.

He simply had not then and did not now have room in his

life for a woman as potent as Marnie Roberts. He was a
horseman first and foremost. From the time he was a school-
boy, he'd known what he wanted to do with his life—be the
best possible trainer he could be.

He had to make sure Marnie understood—and he understood, too—why things had ended the way they had eight
years ago. He just wished he could find the words to do that.
Hell, he wished he could find the *thoughts* to do that.

"You made me forget things, Marnie, things that I really
needed to remember. And that scared the hell out of me. Little
Joe should have won the Classic. He was by far the best horse
entered in that race. But I didn't give him the attention he
needed and deserved that week, because all I could think
about was you. Hell, when I woke up that morning all I
wanted to do was lie there and look at you, and then wake you
up and make love to you again. If I hadn't left when I did—
the way I did—I might still be lying there in that bed with you,
thinking about nothing else."

"And would that be so terrible?" she asked.

"Of course not," he told her. "But that wasn't why I was in
Del Mar," he repeated. "I was in Del Mar to win a race. That
was my job. And my work was the most important thing to me."

She said nothing for a moment, only studied his face in the
darkness as if looking for the answer to a very important
question. Finally she asked, "And what's the most important
thing to you now, Daniel?"

Wasn't the answer to that obvious? "My work," he
answered automatically.

She nodded slowly. "Of course," she said softly. "That is,
after all, what you do best."

Her comment, too, puzzled him. She made it sound as if
being good at what he did was a bad thing.

She bit her lip thoughtfully, her eyes fixed on his, glimmering in the scant moonlight that was filtering through the window. And damned if Daniel didn't find himself wanting to pull her into his arms and kiss her. But as much as it might have felt as if no time had passed since Del Mar, there were eight years between now and then. And eight years was a long time in the best of circumstances. For Daniel and Marnie, it was virtually a lifetime.

So Daniel turned and started for the door, then halted. He couldn't just walk away and leave things as they were, unsettled. He'd done that eight years ago and regretted it.

"It *was* good to see you again, Marnie," he said softly. And since he was being honest, he added, "I hope we see each other again."

She didn't say anything in response, only stood silhouetted against the window with her arms wrapped around her in a way that made him wonder whether she was doing it because she was cold, or if she just needed something—someone—to hold on to. In either case, Daniel understood. There was an emptiness clinging to him that he suspected would be there for a long time.

* * * * *

THOROUGHBRED LEGACY
coming soon wherever books are sold!

Don't miss the brilliant
new novel from

Natalie Rivers

featuring a dark, dangerous
and decadent Italian!

THE SALVATORE MARRIAGE DEAL

Available June 2008
Book #2735

*Look out for more books
from Natalie Rivers coming soon,
only in Harlequin Presents!*

HP12735

REQUEST YOUR FREE BOOKS!

HARLEQUIN *Presents*

2 FREE NOVELS PLUS 2 FREE GIFTS!

PASSION
GUARANTEED
SEDUCTION

YES! Please send me 2 FREE Harlequin Presents® novels and my 2 FREE gifts (gifts are worth about $10). After receiving them, if I don't wish to receive any more books, I can return the shipping statement marked "cancel". If I don't cancel, I will receive 6 brand-new novels every month and be billed just $4.05 per book in the U.S. or $4.74 per book in Canada, plus 25¢ shipping and handling per book and applicable taxes, if any*. That's a savings of close to 15% off the cover price! I understand that accepting the 2 free books and gifts places me under no obligation to buy anything. I can always return a shipment and cancel at any time. Even if I never buy another book, the two free books and gifts are mine to keep forever.

106 HDN ERRW 306 HDN ERRL

Name	(PLEASE PRINT)	
Address		Apt. #
City	State/Prov.	Zip/Postal Code

Signature (if under 18, a parent or guardian must sign)

Mail to the Harlequin Reader Service:
IN U.S.A.: P.O. Box 1867, Buffalo, NY 14240-1867
IN CANADA: P.O. Box 609, Fort Erie, Ontario L2A 5X3

Not valid to current subscribers of Harlequin Presents books.

Want to try two free books from another line?
Call 1-800-873-8635 or visit www.morefreebooks.com.

* Terms and prices subject to change without notice. N.Y. residents add applicable sales tax. Canadian residents will be charged applicable provincial taxes and GST. This offer is limited to one order per household. All orders subject to approval. Credit or debit balances in a customer's account(s) may be offset by any other outstanding balance owed by or to the customer. Please allow 4 to 6 weeks for delivery. Offer available while quantities last.

Your Privacy: Harlequin Books is committed to protecting your privacy. Our Privacy Policy is available online at www.eHarlequin.com or upon request from the Reader Service. From time to time we make our lists of customers available to reputable third parties who may have a product or service of interest to you. If you would prefer we not share your name and address, please check here. ☐

HP08

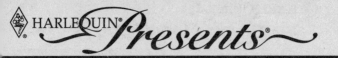

HARLEQUIN *Presents*

**Harlequin Presents brings you
a brand-new duet by star author**

Sharon Kendrick

THE GREEK BILLIONAIRES' BRIDES

Power, pride and passion—discover how only
the love and passion of two women can reunite
these wealthy, successful brothers,
divided by a bitter rivalry.

Available June 2008:

THE GREEK TYCOON'S
BABY BARGAIN

Available July 2008:

THE GREEK TYCOON'S
CONVENIENT WIFE

HP12736

HARLEQUIN *Presents*

EXTRA

TALL, DARK AND SEXY
The men who never fail—seduction included!

Brooding, successful and arrogant, these men
can sweep any female they desire off her feet.
But now there's only one woman they want—
and they'll use their wealth, power, charm and
irresistibly seductive ways to claim her!

**Don't miss any of the titles in this exciting
collection available June 10, 2008:**

*Harlequin Presents EXTRA delivers a themed
collection every month featuring 4 new titles.*